Don't get your Vicars in a Twist

-

The Novel
By
Ann Gawthorpe

Don't get your Vicars in a Twist is based on the play of the same name written by me and Lesley Bown and published by StageScripts. Very popular with amateur dramatic groups, it has had dozens of productions all around the UK as well as in Ireland, Australia, New Zealand and Canada.

It is the first in a series of comic novels called The Kingsford Chronicles centred on the imaginary village of Kingsford. The next one, written by Lesley is called Dandelion and Burdock and will be available on Amazon in Autumn 2021

This story is a work of fiction and any resemblance to anyone, living or dead, is entirely coincidental.

The front cover artwork for the book is courtesy of Stewart Taylor who created it for Studio Theatre's production of 'Don't get your Vicars in a Twist' in 2015. He can be contacted via Instagram @stewtaylor.

Studio Theatre, which is based in Salisbury, celebrates its 70th anniversary in 2022 and now has its own purpose-built 92-seater theatre. Although an amateur drama group, their productions are as good as many a professional company and they have been presented with many awards from winning the Open Stages Competitions run by the Royal Shakespeare Company to the Creative Arts Award run by Wiltshire Life Magazine.

New members are always warmly welcome - whether they want to act, direct or help backstage. Their website is www.studiotheatre.org.uk and further information can be found on the membership page.

Other works by the author
Plays published by StageScripts and co-written with Lesley
Country Dances
Practice to Deceive
Over Exposure
Living Doll
Ashes to Ashes
Whatever you Want

Fiction published by FeedaRead and Amazon
Face to Face
G'day and other Stories co-written with Lesley Bown and Jean Dennis

Non-fiction published by Hodder
Write Your Life Story and get it Published
Creative Writing Masterclass – Writing Plays co-written with Lesley Bown
Get your Articles Published co-written with Lesley Bown

Chapter 1

'And don't forget to pay the caterers.' The words punched their way through the front door and followed George down the path like heat-seeking missiles. He kept his head down as they locked onto a spot between his shoulder blades. His wife was normally easy going, but hot flushes and their third daughter's imminent wedding was proving to be a dangerous combination.

But once he was through the front gate, he straightened his shoulders and adopted his customary urbane manner. Someone had once told him that he looked a bit like Fred Astaire and it was all he could do not to break into a couple of dance steps. Instead, he plucked an early rose growing over his neighbour's garden wall, stuck into his lapel of his grey two-piece suit, licked the blood off his finger and turned right towards the Vicarage.

If all went well today, he would not only have enough money to pay the deposit on the wedding breakfast, but a little extra left over as well. He looked at his watch, five-past-eight on a sunny May morning - perfect. He allowed himself to hum a few bars of Cliff Richard's 'Summer Holiday.' But not too many, after all he was a Church Warden of St Hildegard's, Kingsford, and he had a position to maintain.

At the opposite end of the village, Alan, the other Church Warden was feeding breakfast to his mother's Pekinese. He looked round the kitchen while little Ping snuffled through its dish of prime roast venison – at least that's what it said on the tin - and checked that he had done his chores. He'd already made his bed, changed the bin bag and sprayed air freshener round the bathroom. The washing up was draining and yesterday's newspapers were in the recycling bag, all he had to do was check the calendar for appointments.

He held his breath as he turned over the page. He was certain his mother would have found somewhere for him to take her to. If it wasn't a bowling club coffee morning it would be a visit to her sister two hours up the motorway. For some strange reason his mother was incapable of driving if Alan was there to run her around. He knew nothing had been pencilled in when he'd looked the evening before, but his mother had been known to creep down at three-o-clock in the morning and add a last-minute demand such as picking up the dry cleaning or taking her for a walk along the sea front at Weston-super-Mare.

The square allotted to Saturday was blank. He blinked and checked again. No, nothing for him to do, nowhere for him to go, the morning was his.

He quietly opened the back door and tiptoed down the garden path to the shed. He carefully eased open the door, but sadly not carefully enough to stop the rusty squeak. He stopped, poised on one foot and looked back at the bungalow. The back door was opening slightly and then closing again. After two or three attempts it finally opened wide enough to allow Ping to slither through and run towards him, barking loudly. He put his finger across his lips and pleaded with the dog to keep quiet. Ping understood a lot of human sign language, but always ignored it. He jumped up at Alan's legs, wiping gobbets of his breakfast on Alan's trousers and continued barking.

Alan concentrated on his mother's bedroom curtains. If they twitched all would be lost. They remained closed. He shook Ping off his leg and stepped into the shed. When his eyes had adjusted to the gloom, he made his way to the back and picked up a pot plant, which he had smuggled in two days earlier.

He checked it over for signs of damage or greenfly. It was fine. The soil was moist but not waterlogged. The leaves were glossy and the miniature rose buds were just about ready to burst open.

Alan thought his heart was about ready to burst open. Ever since the new Vicar had arrived in Kingsford four weeks ago, he had been in love. Caroline Timberlake, with her long golden curls, blue eyes and dimpled smile, was the first female vicar to be appointed to the diocese, possibly the first in the country, and she was now the incumbent at St Hildegard's.

He picked up the plant and gently dropped it into its bag. He peered round the shed door. Ping was relieving himself behind the lilac bush and from the grunting could be there for some time. Alan eased out of the shed and slid down the side of the house and out through the front gate. He didn't dare take the car as starting the engine would have definitely woken Mother.

Unlike George's front gate, this one didn't act as a psychological barrier. Despite all his precautions as he crossed the little stream, separating the front garden from the High Street, the front door opened. A figure in curlers and a dressing gown stood watching him. 'Don't forget you are taking me shopping at 11-o-clock.'

'But it wasn't on the calendar.' But the door had already closed.

Alan glanced down at the rose bush, it looked as if it was curling up - he knew how it felt. He kept walking.

George thought Kingsford was looking quite picturesque in the May sunshine. The stream sparkled as it meandered under its bridges and the village green had been freshly mowed, scattering the scent of cut grass across the village. It was just the sort of day to take a stroll, which was why he was walking, after all he had plenty of time to check that all was well at the Vicarage, then stroll back home to pick up his car later.

He breathed in deeply and then pulled his stomach in as he nodded to a group of villagers standing outside the Post Office waiting for it to open. With a bit of luck, he would be back there soon with a few pounds to pay into his private savings account.

It didn't seem possible that he was actually going to pull off his audacious plan. When the last vicar had left for pastures new, or rather an inner-city parish to get away from the mud, lack of street lights and noisy cockerels, George had seen an advert in the local paper. A travelling theatrical group wanted a venue to stage a murder mystery weekend.

The requirements were at least eight double bedrooms for the guests, a dormitory for the actors and two to three reception rooms. Kingsford's large, draughty Victorian Vicarage would be perfect, and it would be empty for many weeks if not months until a new Vicar could be found. But the best part was the money being offered - it would pay the deposit on a sit-down meal for eighty guests plus champagne. The original deposit money had been safely lodged in his bank account, until, in a moment of weakness, he had used it to pay for the membership of a very exclusive golf club.

He'd immediately phoned the proprietor of the company, Dickie Wilson, and the date was set. Finding caterers who could provide all the meals hadn't been so easy. He couldn't afford the ones who would be doing his daughter's wedding and, in any case, they couldn't be too local or some gossiping busy body might realise what he was doing and contact the Bishop. In George's experience bishops were best avoided.

And with good reason because it was Bishop Herbert who'd almost put paid to George's plans. Determined to be the first diocese to appoint a female vicar, instead of saving on a salary and leaving the village vicar-free for months as was normal, he'd found and installed Caroline Timberlake within a few weeks of the Reverend Brown leaving. George was horrified.

But fate stepped in. Caroline had no sooner arrived than she said she had to go away for a weekend - a long-standing arrangement which couldn't be broken. George could scarcely breathe when she asked him to hold the fort for her. He waited, adrenalin pooling at the bottom of his stomach. When she gave him the date it was all he could do not to punch the air. By some miracle he wouldn't have to cancel his little scheme - she would be out of the way for two whole days and would never know anything about it.

While the Vicarage was empty, and before Caroline was appointed, he'd already made up the beds in the spare rooms, found mattresses for the attic and invested in duvets and blankets from some charity shops in Bristol where nobody knew him.

As he walked down the road, avoiding the mud, he thanked his lucky stars that he had left everything in place.

The scene was set – what could possibly go wrong.

The wind ruffled Dickie's hair as he tore down the M32 in his open-top Morgan. He sang along to the radio, oblivious to his lack of talent in that field. The sun was shining and he assumed the birds were singing although he couldn't hear them over the throaty roar of the engine.

Only one thing marred his happiness – would he be able to find the village of Kingsford. He'd studied the maps and was fairly confident he knew where it was, but not totally. And first he had to navigate the chaos which was Bristol.

But all this paled beside the excitement of holding one of his celebrated Murder Mystery weekends in a genuine vicarage. He'd started his little company 'Murders 'R' Us' in a small way; the odd invite to a private house for an evening of mayhem and murder, and a few weekends in different hotels - although he preferred not to think about the one in Eastbourne. But most of his business came from fundraisers in pubs and birthday parties in village halls.

He had a group of actors he could call upon and for this weekend he had picked two has-beens who were desperate to take any kind of work; a resting actor; a guy who claimed to have done something on television, which no one had seen, and two youngsters not long out of drama school who were desperate to get any kind of work, no matter how trivial. What they all had in common was they were cheap and knew the plot if not their lines.

Oh yes, 1994 was going to be his best year yet.

Chapter 2

George paced up and down the Vicarage hall, trying not to step on the joins between the black and white tiles. He couldn't afford any bad luck this weekend. He looked at his watch. What the devil was Caroline doing up there? If she didn't go soon it would hardly be worth her while going at all. He hoped she wasn't poking around in the other bedrooms.

When he'd arrived at the Vicarage half an hour ago, he'd expected her to be long gone, she'd said yesterday she wanted to get an early start. And here she was, fiddling around, and he still had to do a last-minute check. For a start he needed to move all Caroline's stuff out of her bedroom. It was the only one of the eight which had an *ensuite* and Dickie had insisted it was available.

'Come on, come on. You can't have forgotten anything else,' he muttered to himself. The woman had the memory of a gnat; she'd already gone back for her wash bag, her scarf and her spare pair of glasses.

He glanced up as he heard footsteps on the stairs and saw Caroline carrying another suitcase. How much stuff did she need for a weekend away with friends?

'Sorry, George, I'd forget my head if it wasn't screwed on.'

He forced a smile and bowed his head. 'No problem at all Vicar…off you go then.' Moving quickly to the front door, he opened it and took the cases from her. He was halfway through with them when he realised she wasn't following him.

'I just want to say I really do appreciate everything you and Alan do for me, George.'

'Think nothing of it, Vicar, just doing our duty.'

'No, it's more than that. I know I've only been here two or three weeks, but I feel we've all become really good friends.'

'Absolutely Vicar, couldn't agree more. I'll just put these in your car.' He took another step through the front door, but Caroline pulled him back and took one of the cases off him.

'Now, have I got everything? I'd better just check.' She put the suitcase on the hall table, spilling church magazines onto the floor, and started riffling through the contents. George tried not to stare at the frilly underwear and surreptitiously checked his watch instead.

'I wonder if I ought to take another, warmer jumper.'

He could see she was half turning towards the staircase. This was the last straw. 'No!' he shouted. She looked at him, startled. 'I mean, no, Vicar, you won't need another jumper, the forecast is good for this weekend.' Averting his head, he pushed the clothes back into her suitcase and closed it.

Then he threw her coat over her shoulder, opened the front door and tried to push her through it. She could carry her own cases to the car now, he needed to get on. 'Enjoy your reunion. Bye.'

But she ducked under his arm and came back into the hall 'Photos!'

'Photos?'

'Yes, very important, that's why I'm going…to show the others my photos of the ordination. Now where did I put them?' She looked vaguely round the hall. George did the same, he couldn't see any photos.

'I know, they're upstairs.'

George started pacing again and looking at his watch. In his stress, he trod on several joins this time, which did not auger well.

A ring on the front door bell made him jump, he cautiously opened it a crack and peered round. He'd never met Dickie Wilson, but he was pretty certain that the man wearing a cape, mustard waistcoat, bow tie and tweed trilby must be him. 'Sorry, you're too early.' He tried to close the door.

But Dickie was too old a hand to be shut out. He stuck his foot in the gap, forced it open and slid in. 'The early bird catches the worm, old love. Anyway, you said nine-o-clock.'

George tried to push him back out. 'It's ten minutes to and I'm not quite ready for you…'

There was a brief tussle which Dickie won. He looked round the hall, taking in a painting of St Hildegard's and a copy of the 'Stag at Bay' hanging on the walls. His gaze alighted on a couple of diocesan newsletters left on the table, drifted down to the newsletters scattered across the floor and finally settled

14

on a pile of old hymn books stacked on a wooden settle along one wall.

'Oh yes perfect.' And adopting a theatrical pose, he declaimed, 'She was only a vicar's daughter, and her eyes were sparkling blue…' Then evading George's attempt to quiet him, he said, 'Wonderful acoustics, wonderful,' and dropped his two holdalls on the floor.

The phone ringing made them both jump, George stared at it wondering what to do. Dickie stared at George wondering when he was going to answer it. They might have remained like that for some time if a muffled voice hadn't been heard from upstairs.

'Can you answer it George? I'm under the bed.'

Dickie's raised eyebrows implied something very deviant was going on. 'George?'

'It's…it's the cleaner…she's just finishing the bedrooms for you.'

'Ah good, I'll just pop upstairs and have a quick word with her. One of our actors is allergic to furniture polish.'

George grabbed him. 'It's all right, I'll tell her.'

The phone continued to ring. 'George, did you hear me.' Caroline's voice sounded even more muffled.

'It's no problem old love. You answer the phone.' Dickie tried to move towards the stairs but George was hanging on for grim death.

'No, you can't…she doesn't like people watching her work - tricks of the trade and all that. Why don't you wait in here Mr Wilson?' He swung Dickie round and through the door into the drawing room before the luvvie could blink, and quickly locked it.

Then he lunged for the phone almost falling over Dickie's holdalls. 'Kingsford Vicarage...I know I have to pay them today. You reminded me at breakfast and as I was walking out the door.' Out of the corner of his eye he saw Caroline coming down the stairs carrying a large photo album. 'Goodbye.' And he put the phone down.

Scarcely drawing breath, he picked up Dickie's holdalls and held them behind his back. 'Ah, you found them, Vicar.'

'Yes. Was that call for me?'

'Ah no, it was my wife, in a little bit of a panic about the wedding.'

'Busy time eh?'

'Yes...and expensive.'

She tucked the album under her arm and waited for George to pick up her cases. 'Right, well off I go then.'

He stayed put, but smiled and nodded. 'Yes...so...goodbye Vicar.'

'I know you and Alan are taking the morning services on Sunday, but you will be able to keep an eye on the Vicarage as well won't you George, I don't really like leaving it empty.'

George noticed the drawing room door handle was moving up and down and eased across the hall to stand in front of it. 'No problem there, Vicar, it won't be left empty...because, because I shall be calling in several times a day.'

'Bless you, George.' She picked up her cases and moved to the front door and waited for him to open it for her. George stayed firmly put, smiling through gritted teeth – the holdalls were getting heavier and heavier. The impasse was broken by a loud banging.

'What's that noise, George?'

'What noise? I didn't hear anything.'

'It sounded like someone banging on the door.'

George kicked backwards against the panels. 'Oh, that noise that was me, my foot slipped.

'No, it came from inside the room.'

There was a violent rattling of the door handle and a muffled voice shouted, 'Hello, anyone there?'

Caroline dropped her cases. 'There's someone in there.' She stood in front of George and gave him one of her 'Vicar knows best' looks.

George sought inspiration. 'It's…the cleaning lady.'

'That didn't sound like a woman to me. What's going on George?'

'And a man, he's cleaning too. Yes… there's two of them a man and a woman, both cleaners. Don't worry I'll sort them out.'

'I didn't know anything about cleaners coming in. What are they doing here?'

George slumped - would she never stop asking questions. 'They're… they're a surprise…for when you come back.' He hoped Dickie would keep quiet - no such luck

'Hello, I'm stuck in.'

'He's says he's stuck in, George.'

'Yes… stuck in… to the work. He's such an enthusiast.'

The banging got louder and more frantic.

'He's awfully noisy.'

'He's probably giving those rugs a good seeing to.'

Caroline put her hand out to open the door, 'Perhaps I'd better have a word, those rugs are rather valuable.'

'No!' He hadn't meant to shout quite so loudly. 'No, I mean, he's a specialist, he knows what he's doing. Besides, you'll be late, Vicar.' Please just go, he thought, I can't hold these bags much longer. What the hell has the man got in them?

To his relief Caroline suddenly looked at her watch and picked up her cases again. 'Oh goodness, look at the time. I'll leave you to deal with them then George. But thank you it's a lovely idea.'

For a moment George thought she was going to kiss him on the cheek. But she headed for the front door.

'I'll be back by five on Sunday, ready to take Evensong. You will you lock up behind you, won't you?'

'Yes, yes. Goodbye, Vicar, drive carefully. And don't worry I'm locking the front door as soon as you've gone.'

George watched, smiling encouragement as Caroline struggled to get her suitcases out of the front door. When it finally closed, he dropped the holdalls, checked his arms hadn't been stretched and opened the drawing room door. 'So sorry about that Mr Wilson, the door must have got jammed.'

'Now look, I don't want my ruddy punters getting stuck in there.' Dickie gave the handle a couple of violent wiggles.

'Don't worry, I'll see to it.' George straightened his shoulders and clasped his hands together as if in prayer.

'Now, would you like to take your bags upstairs? The cleaners have just gone.'

But Dickie was in no hurry to leave the hall and wandered round, picking up hymn books, putting the magazines back on the table and humming 'All Things Bright and Beautiful' under his breath. 'What a lovely old place. You can breathe the atmosphere,' and he filled his lungs to capacity, arms raised in a blessing.

George didn't care about atmosphere he just wanted to be paid. 'And then perhaps we can talk about the money….'

Dickie looked pained at being pulled out of his reverie. 'Ah yes, the church funds -

I'll settle up later old love. I don't suppose the roof is going to fall in before lunchtime, eh?' He roared with laughter at his own joke.

George didn't. 'How much later, I need it…to take to the bank.' A thought suddenly struck him; Caroline said she'd be back by five, earlier than he'd hoped. 'You will be out of well before five pm, won't you?'

Dickie flicked through one of the newsletters. 'Now don't you worry your little head about that; we always have the denouement after Sunday lunch. The punters all sit there clutching a sherry and pretending to be Hercule Poirot. Then a spot of tea and cakes and off they toddle as happy as larks.'

'And they really don't know which are the actors and which are other guests?' George couldn't believe anyone could be that stupid. But then they must be a bit dim to take part in a murder mystery weekend in the first place. Nothing would get him involved with one.

'Of course, they don't know… apart from the murder victim of course. They usually work out he's an actor. If he isn't, we've made a horrible mistake.' Again, he laughed at his own joke.

Again, George didn't see the joke. 'There won't be any mess will there?'

'Oh yes, there'll be blood everywhere, buckets of stuff. The punters love it.'

George felt his own blood draining away. 'Ah, no blood Mr. Wilson.'

'No blood! You can't have a murder mystery weekend without blood, old love. It would be like mustard without cress or Torville without Dean.'

'No, I'm sorry, I can't have blood on the rugs; they're very valuable. Can't you put something down?'

'Course we can't.'

Dickie suddenly pulled a gun out of his pocket and George put his hands up, then realising it wasn't real, he pretended to scratch his head instead.

'The murderer isn't going to say "hold this gun a minute old chap, I just want to chuck a bit of polythene down before I shoot you". That sort of thing tends to spoil the tension.'

'That's a, er, very convincing replica.'

'Yes, the props have to be realistic.' He handed the gun to George who quickly put it on the hall table with the newsletters.

'But if it's only make-believe….'

'It's got to be plausible, that's what the punters pay for. So, if you can't fulfil your contract, I shall have to revise the fee.'

'But I…the church fund needs it.'

'No blood - no money. You could call your fee blood money.' Dickie laughed uproariously at his own joke.

George didn't. 'This is outrageous.'

'Look, George. You don't mind if I call you George do you, old love? There won't be any lasting mess I promise you - it's only stage blood. Now, have you managed to get us some good caterers?'

George knew when he was beaten. He just hoped the blood stains wouldn't show. He pulled a brochure out of his breast pocket. 'I've booked 'Meals-on-the-Move'. It's all in there. Now if you could pay me straight away, I do have….'

Dickie ignored the brochure. 'I'd rather like to unpack first. The attic is ready isn't it?' and picking up his holdalls he added, 'I assume it's up there.'

As soon as he'd disappeared up the stairs George remembered he still hadn't moved Caroline's clothes out of her bedroom. He was about to rush after Dickie when he saw the gun lying invitingly on the table. He looked at the stairs and then at the gun. He picked it up and pushed it into his belt. Then he tried a few quick draws. Had it been a real gun he would have castrated himself at least twice.

He was in the process of blowing non-existent smoke from the end of the barrel when the front door opened and he saw a figure with his hands above his head holding a wilting pot plant.

Chapter 3

Doing a steady thirty-five miles an hour down the southbound carriage of the M5, Ms Freda Andrews glared at the lorries forced to overtake her as she hogged the inside crawler lane. One driver even had the temerity to shake his fist and shout at her to get off the road. But she had glared right back - she had as much right to be there in her bright red Reliant Robin as they did.

Not that she really wanted to be heading towards Bristol; it was all the fault of her niece Barbara. She glanced across at her sister who was clutching her seatbelt and mouthing prayers. What on earth had possessed Barbara to pay for a weekend in a hotel in the West Country for them both when they would have preferred to celebrate Angela's birthday with their annual dinner at the 'Fox and Goose'.

And she hadn't liked the way Barbara kept trying not to laugh when she waved them off at seven-o-clock in the morning.

She straightened her shoulders and glared at Angela. 'Oh, do cheer up - we're supposed to be on holiday.' Really, Angela was getting more pathetic with the passing years. But then she'd never had to go out to work and fend for herself. As soon as she could Angela had found an easy-going husband who insisted she stay at home. Which she happily did producing one daughter - and not much else.

Not like me thought Freda, I had to work my way up the ladder. And it had been tough teaching in some of those comprehensives. But those years had put steel into her backbone for her final post, as headmistress of a small private prep school. No parent, however rich or pompous, had ever intimidated her. In fact, it was the other way round, they may have stormed into the school with some minor complaint concerning their darling offspring, but they always left with their tails between their legs, grateful that Ms Freda Andrews would continue to allow their wretched child to remain.

She saw a motorway service station sign coming up and, although she deplored the food and beverages on offer in such places, she did need to use the facilities. The map showed that they were only a few miles from Kingsford but Freda didn't quite trust maps. It could be sometime before they were safely unpacked in their room.

As soon as Master Robin Reliant was parked in the Gordano Services Angela stopped praying and the colour came back into her cheeks. She venerated her late father's memory as much as Freda, but she failed to understand why her sister refused to part with his decrepit three-wheeler and insisted on driving it on long journeys.

She was desperate for a cup of coffee, but wasn't sure if Freda would allow her to have one, as within half-an-hour of drinking it she would need the ladies.

But she was in luck. A tail wind meant they had made good time and Freda was happy to spend a while, glaring at various groups of people who were getting off one coach only to get on an even larger one for some reason. So, Angela was able to enjoy a large cappuccino with chocolate on top – and pay a second visit to the loo.

Having less of a good time was the lorry driver who had shaken his fist at them. Somewhere between Sedgemoor Services and junction 22 he failed to notice that the oil tanker in front of him was spilling its cargo. He went into a graceful spin, pirouetted across the three lanes and hit the central barrier.

No one was hurt, but his load of ball-bearings was spread across both sides of the M5, helped on their way by the oil slick. Traffic was diverted onto country roads which were already suffering from endless road works. The result was total gridlock in an area covering large parts of Avon and Somerset.

Caught in the gridlock, like a fly in amber, was a small blue van with gold lettering on its sides: 'Meals-on-the-Move, Highbridge'. Meals-going-Nowhere would better describe its situation.

When he saw the pot plant, George hurriedly pushed the gun down his trousers. 'Alan!'

'George!' Alan slowly lowered his hands and the colour returned to his cheeks. 'What are you doing with a gun?'

'It's not mine…it's a present…for my nephew. What are you doing here?'

'I might very well ask the same question of you.'

'I'm....just checking up that everything's okay while the Vicar's away.'

Alan looked at his pot plant. 'That's exactly what I'm doing.'

'You never said you were going to.'

'If it comes to that, neither did you.'

'Well, as you can see everything is fine.' And George tried to push Alan out the door.

But Alan slipped round him and headed towards the kitchen. 'I'll just find something to stand this on.' George grabbed his arm. 'Don't worry, I'll do it.'

Alan stared at him in amazement. Was George up to something? 'No, it's my plant, I'll do it.'

'Is that for Caroline?'

'Yes, I thought it would be a surprise for her when she comes back tomorrow.' Alan looked at the wilting rose, perhaps it wouldn't be such a nice surprise - he hoped it would perk up before Sunday evening, 'And while I'm here I'll mend the dripping tap for the Vicar.'

'I've already done it.'

Now Alan knew he was right to be suspicious. George wouldn't know a pair of pliers from a pulpit.

George nodded towards the plant, 'You really fancy her, don't you?'

Fancy her - Alan would have died for her. 'Who, Caroline?'

'Yes, Caroline our attractive new vicar.

'I…I think she's umm...well…she's ahhh….'

'Of course she is…and more. And she'll be home on Sunday so come back then.'

They glared at each other. The stand-off was broken by the phone ringing again.

Alan reached it first. 'Hello, Kingsford Vicarage. Church Warden Alan Palmer speaking…He's what?' His voice rose to a screech. 'Could you hang on a minute?' He put his hand over the receiver and whispered. 'It's Miss Jones, the Bishop's secretary.'

'What does she want?'

'She wants to remind Caroline that Bishop Herbert is visiting her this morning.'

'What! What for?'

'I don't know! What shall I say?'

'Just say she's gone away for the weekend.'

'I can't do that - Caroline must have forgotten. What shall we do?'

George paced up and down, Alan following him as far as the phone cord would allow. He tried to ignore the pain of the gun which has slipped down further than he had intended. He blamed Caroline. 'How could she forget a thing like that? The woman's got a memory like a sieve.'

Alan pointed at the phone. 'Come on, what shall I tell her?'

'Tell her…tell her Caroline's ill.

'I can't say that! That's lying, you tell her.' But George had walked towards the stairs and the cord wouldn't stretch that far. Alan heard the secretary asking if he was still there. He had to say something. 'Alright, so what's she ill with?'

George shrugged. 'I don't know, use your imagination.'

'I haven't got any imagination.'

George waved impatiently at the phone. 'Come on, say something, she's expecting ….'

Before George could finish his sentence, Alan had proudly announced Caroline was expecting. 'Yes, a baby, Miss Jones.'

'A baby? You idiot! I was going to say Miss Jones is expecting an answer.' George started pacing again. 'Now they'll think the Vicar's an unmarried mother.'

Alan thought he was going to faint. 'What shall I do?'

'Tell her it's all been a mistake, Caroline's…had an emergency operation and she can't have any visitors.'

'It's all right, Miss Jones, she's not expecting, she's had an operation so she can't have any more mistakes.' Alan put his hand over the phone, 'I think I got that wrong.'

Chapter 4

Dickie walked along the landing looking for the bathroom. It had been an early start and he shouldn't have had that third cup of coffee. He could see from the large cast iron bath and ancient toilet the room hadn't been touched since the place was built. It also had to serve the other seven bedrooms, spread over two floors, as there was only one *ensuite*. Still, he thought, if the punters want to stay in a genuine Victorian Vicarage then they will have to put up with the lack of plumbing. It will add to the authenticity of the weekend.

He climbed the third staircase up to the attic. It looked bleak and uninviting with mattresses on the floor, covered with duvets, and a few rickety chairs. But more than fine for the actors - it was either this or sleep in their cars.

He picked the most comfortable looking mattress and dropped his holdalls on it to stake his claim. Then he unpacked and hung up the costumes he'd brought with him for the actors. Finally, he dropped a copy of the new script on each mattress. There would probably be a bit of moaning about the changes he'd made, particularly from Charles, but he'd come round in the end, he needed the money.

George choked when he heard Alan tell Miss Jones about Caroline's apparent sterilisation. That bit of gossip would spread like wildfire round the diocese and he'd get the blame. 'Tell her Caroline can't have any visitors at the moment.'

Alan tried to explain again to Miss Jones, made matters worse, and added, 'So probably best the Bishop doesn't come today you do understand don't you.' Then he turned white and put his hand over the phone. 'It's too late, he's probably already left.'

'What! You've got to stop him.'

'What, you've got to stop him Miss Jones.' He turned to George. 'She can't.'

'Not her, you.'

'Me? How?'

'Go and stand at the end of the lane and tell him there's no point in him coming to the Vicarage, the Vicar's not well and she can't see anyone.'

'You tell her I can't cope anymore.' Alan thrust the phone at George who had strayed too close.

George scowled, but put on his best Church Warden voice. 'Hello Miss Jones, George Williams speaking…yes the other Church Warden…What make of car is the Bishop driving?... A red one, well done Miss Jones that narrows it down a bit. Right, Mr Palmer is going to intercept him, goodbye.' He put down the phone. 'See, that's all you had to say. Now go and walk down the lane to the main road and stop him.'

'But what if he insists on seeing her?'

'Say she's highly infectious.'

'Suppose he comes from the other direction? I might miss him?'

'Can't you run up and down the lane?'

'No, I can't, you'd better go and stand at one end and I'll stand at the other.'

George looked anxiously up the stairs. 'It's a bit inconvenient at the moment.'

'It'll be even more inconvenient if he gets as far as here.'

'All right, all right.'

Alan was about to go out the front door when he hesitated. 'What if we both miss him?'

'We'll meet back here at ten-thirty,' George thought that would keep Alan away from the Vicarage long enough for him to get his money and go.

'There's just one thing.'

'Now what?' George was trying to manoeuvre him out of the door.

'I can't remember what he looks like.'

'He's…neither can I, just look out for a red car.'

'There could be loads of red cars.'

'But not one with a bloke in a cope and mitre.'

'Would he be wearing them?'

'Yes, I'm sure he would…for a formal visit. Now come on.' The pain of the gun down his trousers was completely forgotten as they ran down the garden path and out into the road.

George pointed to the left. 'You go that way I'll go the other way.'

'I notice you've taken the shorter route to the main road'

'Stop arguing.'

They set off, but both kept looking back to check that the other one was still walking forward. As soon as Alan had disappeared round a bend George turned round and rushed back towards the Vicarage. He needed to get all Caroline's stuff out of her bedroom before Dickie put some guests in there.

He hadn't got far when he saw Alan walking towards him 'Did you manage to stop him, Alan?'

'No, I thought you had.'

'No.'

'So why are you coming back George?'

'I could ask you the same thing.'

When it was clear that neither of them had seen the Bishop, and that nothing was to be gained by glaring at each other they walked off in opposite directions. Neither noticed a beige Ford Focus slip past them and turn into the Vicarage grounds, weighed down with suitcases and two elderly thespians.

Having satisfied himself over the arrangements in the attic, Dickie decided to check on the caterers. The punters would be expecting decent nosh and he wondered whether it had been wise to leave that side of things to George.

He had only just got down the stairs when the front door was slammed wide open and Marigold Dubois, draped in a faux leopard skin coat, made a dramatic entrance followed by Ronald Harvey struggling with three suitcases and two hat boxes.

'Greetings my children, come in, come in. Welcome to Kingsford Vicarage.'

Marigold gave him two loud air kisses. 'So lovely to see you, Dahling. Just put the cases down there Ronnie. You can take them up later.'

Ronald glared at her but didn't have the breath to make a suitable riposte.

Dickie peered out the door and saw there was no one else in the Ford. 'Where's Charles? Didn't he travel down with you?'

'No, he said he wanted to come on his own. You know he won't travel in the same car as Ronald.'

'I do hope we are not going to have any temper tantrums over the weekend.'

'Not from me you won't, not unless he gets up my nose.' Ronald had collapsed on the settle sending some of the hymn books sliding to the floor.

'Well, just to be on the safe side, there's a ban on alcohol.'

'Absolutely, Dickie, but you won't mind if I have a little drink in my room, will you darling? For the throat, you know.' Marigold patted her neck in case he hadn't understood.

'Yes, I do mind so hand them over, now.'

Marigold glared at him and then pulled a bottle of gin out of her bag.

But Dickie knew her too well. 'Come on Marigold, let's have the rest.' He held out his hand and reluctantly

33

she pulled another out of her coat pocket and gave it to him. He put it on the table with the first one and then held out his hand again. Ronald shook the hat boxes and held them out to Dickie who peered inside and added four more to the collection.

Dickie then turned to Ronald. 'And you as well.'

Ronald quickly concealed the hipflask he had been slurping from. 'On the wagon, dear boy, on the wagon.'

'Good because I've made a few changes to the script.'

'Changes! What changes?' Marigold was always alert when it came to script changes. No one was going to take any lines away from her.

'As it's the first time we've done one of these weekends in a real vicarage I thought we needed to add a touch of gravitas to our little scenario. So, Ronald, I want you to take the part of the Bishop.

'Bishop! What Bishop?'

'Bishop Ronald.'

Ronald stood up and walked about the hall for a few moments trying out some bishop-like moves. 'Yes, well, I suppose that does have a certain ring to it dear boy. But what do I wear?'

'Don't worry, I've got the costume.'

Marigold pushed herself in front of Ronald. 'What about me, Dickie? I hope I'm still Lady Alicia. I feel I bring such emotional depths to that role.'

'This is a murder mystery weekend you silly moo, not Hedda Gabler.' Ronald pushed himself in front of Marigold. 'So, if I'm the bishop, Dickie, who's playing my part, the Honourable Giles Forsythe?'

'Angus Wright, do you know him?'

'No, never heard of him.'

'Done the RSC and a bit of telly. He should be here by now; he's coming down with Ian and Lavinia.'

Marigold pushed in front of Ronald. 'How old is he?'

'Middle thirties.'

'Wonderful, it's time we had someone younger for my lover. Ronald looks more like my father every day.'

'Cow.'

'Has been.'

'Children, enough. I had hoped Charles would be here by now, because the other major change is to his part.'

'Isn't he playing the Reverend Thorn then?' Marigold was on full alert again.

'Yes, except he will be a Reverendess or whatever they are called.

'A what?' Ronald snorted - he couldn't believe his ears.

'I've decided to have a lady vicar, they're all the rage now. So, if he wants his money, he'll have to do it in drag. He's done enough panto, so it shouldn't be difficult.'

'And he doesn't know yet?' For the first time since leaving London Ronald felt his spirits rise.

'No, I thought I'd wait and tell him when he gets here.' Dickie knew if he'd told Charles beforehand, he might not have come.

'Oh well, every cloud has a silver lining...Charles in a skirt.' Ronald snorted again, and realised he might not need whisky to get through the weekend after all. Watching Charles forced to dress as a woman would be enough to dull the pain of two days in this god-forsaken place.

Marigold threw another dramatic pose. 'It would serve you right, Dickie if he turned round and went straight home.'

'I don't think he will; I heard his voice-overs have dried up since he had that bout of laryngitis. So, on that happy note I'll show you to your attic.'

Marigold had been inching towards the table and her gin bottles, but the word attic stopped her in her tracks. She slowly turned to face Dickie and in her best Sybil Thorndyke voice said, 'Did you say…attic?'

'Yes. I'm pleased to say we are fully booked. So, you're all going to have to sleep in the attic.'

'What!'

'It's plenty big enough.'

'Marigold Dubois does not sleep in an…attic.'

'Oh, don't fuss old love. Remember I knew you when you were a chorus girl who kipped in an old minibus with the stage hands.'

Seeing she was getting nowhere with Dickie she stood over Ronald who had slumped back on the settle. 'Ronald, are you just going to sit there and accept these appalling conditions?'

'As long as I've got a bed I don't care.'

She turned back to Dickie. 'Well, I shall want the best attic.'

'There's only one so you'll be sharing.'

'Marigold Dubois doesn't share her room with anyone.'

'Oh, give it a rest Marigold; I'm sure I can fix up some blankets to divide your bit off.'

'Just because you don't want anyone to see you take your teeth out.' Ronald couldn't resist it although he knew he'd pay for that remark later.

'Bastard.'

'Backstabber.'

'Oh, and there's only one bathroom so that's for the punters. You'll all have to use the outside loo.'

That got Ronald to his feet. 'I say Dickie that's going a bit too far.'

This time it was Marigold who snorted. 'After all Ronald does have a weak bladder.'

'Whore.'

'Ham.'

With both of them glaring at him Dickie decided it would be politic to back down. 'Okay. You can use the downstairs cloakroom. But remember, the punters have paid good money for this weekend and I expect you to act like professionals.'

Ronald looked at his watch. Just gone ten-o-clock! He needed his caffeine kick. 'I could murder a cup of coffee.'

'I don't know if the caterers have arrived yet. I was just on my way to check.'

'Well, don't expect me to do any cooking.'

'Yes, spare us Marigold's attempts go poison us.'

'Tosser.'

'Tart.'

Dickie was beginning to wish he hadn't asked them to come. Sometimes it didn't do to save money. At least the rest of the cast could be relied on not to let him down. 'The guests will be arriving soon so run along.'

'So how does one get to this…garret?' Marigold looked mutinous.

'Up two flights of stairs, turn right at the top, go along the corridor and then up the next flight straight ahead.'

'I shall go up first and choose the best bed. Ronald you may bring my cases.' She started walking up the stairs expecting Ronald to follow her, but he stayed where he was.

'Do I still get murdered in the drawing room, Dickie?'

'No.'

'Well, where then?' Ronald couldn't always remember from the script what he was supposed to say or where he was supposed to be and it made him testy.

'You're the Bishop, remember, you don't get murdered at all. Well, not unless you annoy Charles. He's going to murder you one day.'

'Oh yes I forgot, I've been elevated to higher things.'

'Yes, so try to remember that, Ronnie. And none of your usual hanky-panky with the female guests or I shall dock your pay.'

'You can't do that.'

'Watch me.'

Ronald shuffled a bit and glanced up the stairs to make sure Marigold had disappeared. 'Umm, Dickie, dear boy, talking of money, I was wondering, the journey down has left me a bit short, any chance of an advance?'

'None at all. You'll get paid at the end like everyone else.'

Ronald was about to protest when Marigold appeared at the top of the stairs and she wasn't looking pleased.

'Dickie! There's the most appalling draught up here, the wind is literally whistling straight through me.'

'You should try wearing knickers.' Ronald couldn't resist another dig, although he knew he would pay for that later as well.

'Amateur.'

'Trollop.'

Seeing Dickie was looking less than sympathetic Marigold changed her tactics. 'I have to think of my throat, Dickie darling.'

'I told you, I will sort something out. Now, both of you get upstairs before the punters arrive.'

While Dickie was glaring at Marigold, Ronald surreptitiously slid a bottle of gin into his pocket, picked up the suitcases, and headed up the stairs.

Dickie locked the front door. He wanted to welcome his guests personally not have them wandering around. Then he headed towards the kitchen hoping that the caterers had let themselves in the back door.

Chapter 5

Bishop Herbert, the cause of George and Alan's problem, was feeling pleased with himself as he drove across the Mendips in his old but comfortable maroon Rover. He wasn't supposed to be driving after having a few blackouts, but he was keen to see his new vicar and discuss the way forward for women in the church.

He had met Caroline Timberlake when he attended the service in Bristol Cathedral for the first group of women to be ordained into the Church of England. He was so determined to be the first diocese to have one he stood outside afterwards and asked each woman as she came out if they could take over the parish of St Hildegard's. The first three said they had already got somewhere, but Caroline had been thrilled to accept.

Now that she was settled into the parish, he'd asked his secretary to fix date for him to visit her. He knew it would require careful planning and nerves of steel to elude his wife who insisted on acting as his chauffeuse. But there was no way she would agree to drive him to Kingsford. Her views on the ordination of women were shrill and verbose. She had even hidden the car keys to stop him creeping off without her.

So, the first thing he had to learn was how to hot wire a car. He knew it could be done - he'd seen it on the television. But who could teach him? Then he remembered his cousin, the one the family never spoke about.

If Gilbert thought it odd that Herbert was not only ringing him, but asking how to bypass the normal ignition system he didn't query it. Initially he'd suggested Herbert call one of the road-side rescue companies if he was stuck, but Herbert said he didn't belong to any of them and couldn't Gilbert talk him through it on the phone.

Gilbert said that wouldn't work, but he would come to the palace to give him hands-on tuition.

Herbert checked his wife's diary for her next visit to one of the many Young Wives groups in the area and was pleased to find that Gilbert was available on one of the afternoons. 'Come round the back about two-o-clock. Oh, and I also need to break into the car first, my wife has hidden the keys.'

Gilbert arrived with a bag containing numerous bits of wire, clips, wire strippers and duct tape. But the most surprising item was an old tennis ball which he handed to Herbert.

'What am I supposed to do with this?' Herbert bounced the ball a couple of times against the garage wall.

'I'll show you.' Gilbert took the ball back and cut a small slit in it. 'You hold it over the keyhole like this.' He then pressed the ball against the door of the Rover and Herbert was surprised to see the lock spring up on the inside. 'Easier than a coat hanger and less messy than smashing the window.'

Gilbert then showed Herbert how to remove the plastic cover under the steering column to get to a bundle of wires. 'The tricky bit is getting the right ones. Get it wrong and you're in for a nasty shock.'

Herbert could well believe that, there seemed to be a lot of them and how would he know which wire was which. After some trial and error and much swearing Gilbert worked out which ones to use. And after a few practices Herbert could get the Rover started within twenty seconds.

Gilbert then made him solemnly swear that he would never take up car thieving, but would only use his new-found skills for personal use. Herbert suspected this was less about saving him from a life of crime than Gilbert not wanting competition in the luxury car market.

On the morning of the escape Herbert was up early and with thudding heart crept down to the garage with a large bundle under his arm and a thermos flask of coffee – just in case. His blood pressure was so high he thought he might black out before getting back to the kitchen.

After breakfast he put on his oldest gardening clothes and told his wife he would be doing some weeding down by the moat. She looked at him distractedly and said he'd have to get his own lunch because she would be tied up with the Mothers Union business all day.

He made sure she saw him walking past the window and gave her a wave with his trowel. Then he hot footed it to the garage, broke into the Rover, got it started and drove quietly away.

Once he was well clear of the Palace he pulled into a lay by and took out the bundle. He had no intention of meeting Caroline in his dirty jeans and sweatshirt, so had secreted out his best grey suit and purple vest. It wasn't easy changing in the car but if his wife had seen him in his suit, she would have dumped the MU and stuck to him like glue.

He hoped his secretary had remembered to ring Caroline and remind her of his visit - he hadn't dare do it from the Palace in case his wife heard him – but Miss Jones was very reliable, if prone to gossip.

He turned on the radio just in time to hear a local news reader describing the chaos on the roads following an accident on the M5 which was closed in both directions.

He said a prayer for the angry motorists forced to find their way round unfamiliar lanes trying to follow diversions signs which invariably sent them back to the place they started from. Then, tapping his fingers along to Meatloaf singing 'I'd do anything for Love, but not that' he put his foot down.

Endless visits to far-flung parishes in his diocese meant he knew every short cut, back lane and even rarely used cart tracks so he was totally confident he would get to St Hildegard's by coffee time.

Meanwhile, Caroline, the object of his illicit journey, was also feeling sorry for the motorists on the M4 heading west at eighty miles an hour in the opposite direction to her. She knew that within a few miles they would hit the traffic jam which was clogging up the roads round

Bristol. If only there was some way to warn them. But perhaps it was better they didn't know, at least they would have a few more minutes of ignorance. She was a gentle soul and didn't want anyone to suffer.

It had taken her a while to get out of the city herself, and she was cross that she hadn't left earlier. But what did that matter now, the sun was shining and the motorway ahead was fairly free of traffic so it wouldn't take her too long to reach the junction for Oxford.

However, she couldn't quite dismiss the feeling that she had forgotten something, something important. She mentally went through what she needed for the weekend – she had her photo album and a confirmation letter from the hotel she was booked into. The services would be covered by the church wardens and the car was full of petrol – no, she was sure she hadn't forgotten anything.

She turned on the radio, but nothing appealed to her. So, she resolutely pushed the vague worries aside and thought about the group for friends she was meeting up with.

They had all attended the same theological college in Oxford, but since taking their degrees had dispersed around the country. But the happy memories of their time together in that city made it the obvious place for the reunion.

Chapter 6

George waited ten minutes this time before rushing back to the Vicarage, reasoning Alan would be too far away to see him. He threw himself at the front door and bounced straight off. Who the hell had locked it? Ignoring the pain in his shoulder he rushed down the side of the house and in the back door.

Where he came face to face with Dickie. 'Ah, Mr Wilson....'

'Dickie, please.'

'Dickie...yes. I just need to check on one of the bedrooms...make sure it's up to scratch for your guests.'

'Good. But first where are the caterers? As you can see the kitchen is strangely empty.'

George looked round. He couldn't argue with Dickie's observation. But before he could say anything the back door burst open and Alan staggered in breathless and not a little muddy. 'Did you get rid of him?'

'Who?'

'The Bishop, isn't that why you're here? I saw you over the hedge running back and,' He stopped when he saw Dickie, who held out his hand.

'Hello, am I glad to see you.'

Alan stared at Dickie in a mixture of horror and amazement. He didn't look like a Bishop. He didn't sound like a Bishop. But he was here and that was a disaster. He shook Dickie's hand. 'Good morning sir it's...it's nice to meet you.'

'So, do you need any help bringing in the food?'

Alan looked at George for help. Were they supposed to provide lunch or something? 'Food?'

'You are the caterers, aren't you?'

'No, I'm Alan Palmer the...,' but before he could say anything else George had swung him round towards the back door.

'Mr Palmer is off to meet someone. And it wouldn't do to keep him waiting, would it, Alan?' With that he gave Alan a sharp shove outside, shut the door and locked it.

'About these caterers George, I hope there isn't going to be a problem.'

'No, no, they should be here any minute.'

Dickie gave him a speculative look, but decided against pursuing the topic. 'Okay, I'll just check the rugs in the drawing room as you are so worried about the blood.'

George started to follow him, but he could hear Alan hammering on the back door and didn't want Dickie to come back and start asking questions. He opened it a crack. 'What do you want? Have you seen the Bishop?'

'No, I thought that man was him.' Alan pushed the door open and looked round the kitchen. 'But, if he's not the Bishop who is he?'

George looked heavenwards until inspiration struck, 'He's checking for woodworm.'

'Woodworm! What woodworm?'

'The Vicar thought she saw woodworm in the library panelling.'

'I don't believe it.'

'Well, you know what women are like. Now go and stop the Bishop.' He was about to manhandle Alan out of the door again when Dickie poked his head into the kitchen.

'It's okay they won't get stained, but I'll move them to be on the safe side.'

Alan glared at George and George prayed for inspiration. 'He's…staining the floorboards.'

'What about the woodworm?'

'He's doing them as well.'

'He's going to stain the woodworm?'

'No, the floorboards, he's killing the woodworm. Try and keep up Alan.'

'There's something odd going on here,' and Alan was out of the kitchen and into the hall before George could stop him.

'Look, I didn't want to have to tell you Alan.'

'Tell me what?'

George looked round the hall for help, but none came. 'Isn't it obvious?'

'No.'

'I would have thought it was.'

'Well, it isn't.'

George looked round the hall again and noticed a small crack above the window. 'Look up there, that crack, there's a structural fault in the Vicarage. In fact, it's probably not safe for you to stay here a moment longer.'

He unlocked the front door and tried to push Alan out, but Alan was immovable.

'It's not a very big crack; I could fill that in myself.'

'You work in insurance Alan you're not qualified to make that judgement. No this needs an expert - so off you go.'

'Hang on, is that bloke a surveyor as well?'

'Yes, a surveyor, that's right…and he says the whole place is in dangerous state and could crumble about our ears at any minute.'

'It's the first I've heard about it.'

'I didn't want to worry you with the problem.'

'But it's as solid as a rock, look.' Alan banged loudly on the wall next to the drawing room door, and like a genie from the lamp Dickie popped out with two rugs under his arms.

'Did you knock?'

'Yes, how long will it take to solve the problem?'

Dickie looked confused then his face cleared, 'As I said to George, it'll be sussed by Sunday lunch.'

'You're very confident.'

'Well, there are plenty of clues about old love.' He turned to George. 'I'll put these in the utility room, shall I?'

'There you are you see, Alan, nothing for you to worry about, so off you go.' Once again, he tried to get Alan out of the front door.

Once again Alan was immovable. 'What sort of clues?'

Dickie turned in the kitchen doorway. 'Well, the body's a bit of a give-away for a start.'

Chapter 7

Alan stared at the kitchen door through which Dickie had disappeared. 'Body! What does he mean by the body George?'

'Ah…a rat, there's a rat's body in the cellar.'

'Rats?'

'Yes, the place is riddled with them.'

'We need a pest exterminator then. Where's the Yellow Pages?' Alan started rummaging in the table drawer. 'There should be one in here.'

George slammed the drawer shut catching Alan's fingers in it. 'It's okay Mr Wilson knows how to deal with them. Now will you go and look for the Bishop.'

Normally Alan would have made a fuss about his wounded digits, but love of Caroline acted as a powerful anaesthetic. 'I don't know, as joint Church Warden I think I should stay here and check on this Mr Wilson…for Caroline.'

'Right, fine, stay if you want,' George shrugged, 'we'll just let the Bishop walk in and find Caroline's away enjoying herself and has completely forgotten all about him.'

'But….'

'You obviously don't care if Caroline gets into trouble.' He could see Alan was wavering. Taking

50

advantage, he gave a final push and Alan was outside and the front door firmly shut.

He needed to get upstairs, but he also needed to move the gun which was now causing considerable pain. It had nearly crippled him running back to the Vicarage. With a sigh of relief, he pushed his hand down the front of his trousers and tried to pull it out. Unfortunately, it got jammed in his boxer shorts.

As he struggled, he heard footsteps coming down the stairs and looked over his shoulder. Marigold might be a bit long in the tooth but to a church warden living at the back of beyond she was an exotic vision of loveliness. He stared mesmerised by her tousled, tawny locks, long sweeping eyelashes, gleaming white teeth, ample heaving bosom and curvaceous derriere. What he didn't know was it all came off, or out at night to be carefully arranged by her bedside.

Marigold hesitated then decided the man must be the new actor Angus. 'Oh, hello darling, you must be my new lover.'

That caused George to straighten up in a hurry, so he pushed the gun further down and spun round. 'What!' Surely, he'd misheard?

'I must say you look older than I was told, but anyone's better than Ronnie. Do you want to practice?' And with one swift and skilful move she pulled George into her arms.

'Practice!' His voice came out in a high-pitched squeak, which wasn't surprising considering where the gun now rested.

'Well, we haven't met before so it will be easier if we try a few kisses first. I'm Marigold Dubois by the way.' Then she kissed George passionately.

Once the feeling of being suffocated by an amorous octopus had worn off George found he was enjoying it. Neither saw Alan come back in the front door.

Marigold finally broke the clinch. 'Oh, is that a present in your pocket or are you just pleased to see me?'

Nothing like this had ever happened to George before, but what the hell he was up for it. 'That's for me to know and you to find out.'

Marigold slid his jacket down over his shoulders. 'Oh, I knew we would get on.'

Alan had seen enough. 'George, what are you doing?'

George jumped and pushed Marigold away. 'You've made a horrible mistake, Madam, I'm a respectably married man.'

'I made a mistake all right. I mistakenly thought you could act.' Marigold snatched up two of the bottles of gin and walked up stairs with as much dignity as she could.

'George, who's that woman?'

George struggled to get his jacket back in place. 'She's…She's helping Mr Wilson, she's his assistant.'

'So why was she kissing you?'

'I…kissing me? George was now properly dressed and back in control. 'No, it may have looked like that, but I had something in my eye and she was trying to remove it.'

'That wasn't the only thing she was trying to remove.'

'Did I hear her ladyship?' Dickie asked, coming out of the kitchen minus rugs.

Unless the house had suddenly filled up with sex-starved women, George assumed he meant the woman who'd kissed him. 'Yes, she's gone back upstairs.'

'I suppose she's still trying to find something wrong with the attic.' He went over to the table. 'And she's taken some gin bottles with her.' He picked up the rest. 'Well, she's not having anymore. I saw a useful cupboard in the dining room with a lock.' And he disappeared with them.

Alan waited until Dickie had shut the door and then turned to George, 'Her ladyship! You said she was his assistant.'

'She is...it's a very high-class firm.'

'So, what's wrong with the attic?'

George didn't think he could cope with much more. Once again, he looked at the ceiling for inspiration. 'The roof leaks.'

'And I suppose you're going to tell me she's catching the drips in a gin bottle.'

'Yes, no. Never mind the attic; you should be outside, stopping the Bishop.'

Alan's shoulders drooped, 'Oh, what's the point, George, he's never going to believe Caroline's ill. We have to ring Caroline and get her to come straight back. She gave me the hotel number.' Alan pulled a scrap of paper out of his pocket and lifted up the receiver.

George had never moved so fast in his life. 'No, you can't.' He whipped the phone away from Alan and clutched it to his chest.

'Why?'

Questions, always endless questions, he thought his head would burst. 'Because… because…the place needs fumigating.' He relaxed his grip on the phone, yes that was a good one. 'That's why she's gone away, to get away from the fumes. She's allergic to them. So, she can't come back until Sunday evening.'

'I thought it was a college re-union.'

'And that as well.' Before George could elaborate there was a loud bang, a lot of swearing and the dining room door burst open to show Dickie struggling with a large screen, the kind women get undressed behind in second-rate movies. No one had ever found out which Vicar had brought it to the Vicarage - or why.

Alan was the first to break the silence. 'Where are you going with that?'

'I'm putting it in the attic.'

'Ah…because of the fumes?'

'No, because if I don't, I'll have a riot on my hands.'

'A riot!'

George forced himself to laugh merrily. 'Riot? No, he said dry rot. Isn't that right Dickie, the screen's got dry rot?'

'Has it? It looks fine to me.' Dickie dropped the screen to take a closer look at the wooden frame. All the love in world couldn't stop the pain Alan felt when it landed on his foot.

54

'There you are Alan, nothing to worry about, the screen is fine.' And taking advantage of Alan's incapacity George once again tried to push him out the front door. 'So off you go.'

But Alan was having none of it and hopped across to Dickie. 'I must say Mr Wilson I'm most impressed with your talents. Do you have a brochure or leaflet about your company?'

George pulled him away. 'No, he doesn't it's all done by word of mouth.'

'Yes, of course I have, here you are.' Dickie pulled a leaflet out of his pocket, passed it to Alan, then picked up the screen and struggled with it up the stairs.

Despite George's best efforts to take it from him, Alan hopped across the hall, sat on the settle and started reading. 'Murders 'R' Us'! Good grief George, what is he, the Mafia?'

Alan turned the leaflet over and studied it. 'Intrigue, blackmail, crimes of passion! What the hell's going on George? And don't try to tell me he's an agony aunt as well.'

'It's just a catchy name. For a pest exterminator.'

George tried to snatch it but Alan proved to be surprisingly agile despite his damaged foot and moved out of reach. 'I want to read this. "Are you the next Miss Marple or Sherlock Holmes? Can you fish out the clues from the red herrings? Our murder mystery weekend in Kingsford Vicarage will provide chills and thrills at a very reasonable price".' Alan looked up slowly and stared at George. 'Why does it say Kingsford Vicarage?'

George shrugged

'Have you said this company can use the Vicarage?'

'I may have done, sort of.'

'Are you mad?'

'Look, I need the money. Have you any idea how much weddings cost these days? I've already forked out for two and now the wife's insisting the youngest has to have the same as the others. I mean the flowers alone….'

'Does the Vicar know?'

'The cost of weddings? I expect so.'

'No, that you've hired out the Vicarage.'

'I may have mentioned it, in passing.'

'She doesn't know, does she?'

George ignored this and spread out his hands to show that what he was doing was eminently reasonable. 'Look, it was empty when I said Dickie Wilson could have it. How was I to know the Bishop was going to appoint a new vicar so quickly? It usually takes months. And talking of bishops, shouldn't you be out there trying to stop him?'

'On one condition, George, you must cancel this weekend.'

'I can't, I signed a contract.'

'So, break it.'

George looked at him, Alan wouldn't want to break a contract if he'd signed it. 'We both signed it.'

'We! Like you and me.'

'In a manner of speaking.'

'You forged my signature?'

'Sort of.'

'That's it. I'm going to ring Caroline.'

'Fine, fine, but some of the money is going to the church roof fund.'

'You should still have told her…and me.'

George shrugged his shoulders and made as if to go out of the front door. 'Okay, ring her and while you're on the phone don't forget to tell her she's pregnant, oops no she's not, she's had a little operation to get rid of her mistake.' He took Alan by the shoulders. 'Oh, come on Alan, it's just one weekend, and Caroline need never know what you've done.'

'What I've done!'

'All we have to do is stop the Bishop and I promise I won't say a word.'

Alan couldn't decide whether it was better to ring Caroline, confess all and hope she'd understand, or not ring her and hope she'd never find out. But before he could reach a conclusion the doorbell rang and then it was too late.

'It's him, he's here.' Alan looked round for somewhere to hide.

George quickly locked the front door to stop the Bishop walking in and hissed at Alan, 'This is all your fault.'

'My fault.'

'We could have stopped him getting this far if you hadn't come creeping back.'

Alan hissed back. 'Me! What about you, you were supposed to be watching out as well.'

There was another even louder ring on the bell.

'What are we going to do, George?'

'Ignore him, perhaps he'll go away.'

But whoever was outside wasn't going away. They started hammering and banging on the door. Dickie appeared at the top of the stairs. 'Is someone at the door?'

Alan and George looked at each other and then at Dickie hoping inspiration would strike.

'Can you deal with them? I've got my hands full at the moment.' And he disappeared.

Alan crept to the door and peered through the letter box.

George leaned over his shoulder. 'What can you see?'

'It looks like an eye.'

Chapter 8

Dickie could hear loud mutterings as he manhandled the screen through the attic door. For all their waspish spats, Ronald and Marigold could always be relied on to present a united front when it came to complaining.

To forestall any moaning, he told Marigold she could use the screen to barricade her end of the attic off. He noticed she had already taken some of the blankets to create a makeshift curtain – he'd have to ask George for some more as it would be easier to get a lion to give up its prey than Marigold to part with the bedclothes.

Then he turned to Ronald and reminded him that work was thin on the ground and that he should be grateful for a job, 'Don't forget you have been elevated to play the Bishop. I could have got someone else to take that part, but you have the gravitas for it, which is why I chose you, but…,' He could see Ronald visibly backing down and adopting a clerical demeaner.

'Well, of course dear boy, I think the role suits me down to the ground.'

Marigold snorted, and pulled the screen alongside her bed. She certainly didn't want Dickie to see the gin bottles she managed to smuggle upstairs.

Dickie opened his suitcase and passed Ronald a purple shirt. 'Here you are My Lord.' Then he took down a brocade cope and gave it a good shake to remove the wrinkles, and then brushed the matching mitre to remove the dust. 'You will have to wear these as well.'

Ronald was positively purring as he tried the cope on for size. If this didn't pull the women nothing would.

Madeleine Forbes could hardly contain her excitement. She had travelled from Reading to Bristol on the train and then taken a taxi. Despite the driver opening the rear door for her she plumped herself in the passenger seat and settled back for a nice chat with him.

'Oh, it's going to be so exciting. I've never been on a murder mystery weekend before, but I have read lots of Agatha Christie so I know there will be lots of red herrings. Do you like crime novels? I'm sure you do. Who's your favourite writer? Mine's Barbara Cartland, but of course she doesn't write detective stories. Oh, I can't wait to get there.'

Neither could the driver who hoped his silence would shut her up for a while, but Maddie, as she introduced herself, didn't need a response. She talked non-stop through Bristol, through the traffic jam on the A370 and through the long crawl behind a tractor spewing mud from its wheels. By the time they reached the Vicarage the driver was ready to commit murder himself.

He shamelessly over charged her and then drove away even though the Vicarage looked empty and normally he waited until his female passengers were safely indoors.

Maddie put her suitcase down and looked at the Vicarage. 'Perfect.' She rang the doorbell and stepped back waiting for her welcome. Dickie Wilson had sounded so charming on the phone and she couldn't wait to meet him. Nothing happened so she tried again. Still nothing. Perhaps the bell wasn't working. She hammered on the door and was sure she could hear voices inside. She bent down and peered through the keyhole. To her surprise an eye was staring back at her. She put her lips to the letter box and called 'Hello, I can see you.'

Alan fell backwards from the door, 'He's seen me.'

'Let me in you naughty things.'

Alan started looking for somewhere to hide again, but George stood his ground.

'That doesn't sound like the Bishop.'

'How do you know? You can't even remember what he looks like?'

'Well, unless he's got his gaiters up too high, I'd say that was a woman.'

While Alan hid under the hall table George opened the door. 'Sorry about that, the door got stuck.'

'Oh, not to worry.' Maddie quickly came in, put her case down and looked round the hall. 'My what a lovely place. I can't tell you how much I'm looking forward to this weekend Mr Wilson.'

'I'm not Mr Wilson.' George stepped past her checking the road outside. 'Are you alone?'

Maddie looked at him archly, 'Why yes, I am.'

George backed away. 'You haven't seen a bishop anywhere, have you?'

'No although I simply adore men of the cloth.'

Alan crawled out from under the table and got creakily to his feet. 'Who are you then madame?'

Maddie turned her attention to Alan. 'Ah, you must be Mr Wilson.'

'No, I'm not, there's no one here by that name.'

George said, 'He's only joking. So, you're here for the weekend?'

'Yes, that's right. I'm Madeleine Forbes, but you can call me Maddie. Now what about you two? Are you guests as well?

'No, we're...,'

Alan's speech was cut short by George clamping his hand over his mouth and finishing the sentence, 'in a bit of a hurry.'

'Well before you rush off, which one of you boys is going to show me to my room?'

Alan pulled George's hand away. 'We can't, you haven't got a room...,'

The hand was immediately clamped back on and George added, 'at the front, they've all been taken, you're at the back.'

'Oh, I don't mind where I sleep.'

'I'm sorry, but I'm afraid we have to dash off.'

'Secret assignations eh. All part of the mystery. How wonderful.'

She watched George frogmarch Alan out of the front door.

'Goodbye - see you later.' She looked round the hall wondering where the receptionist was when Dickie came down the stairs and walked towards her with open arms.

'Hello, you must be Mrs Forbes.' And he kissed her theatrically on both cheeks.

'Yes, that's little old me.'

'Dickie Wilson. We spoke on the phone. Delighted to meet you.'

Maddie clasped his hands. 'I'm so excited Mr Wilson.'

'Dickie, please.'

'And I'm Maddie.'

'Maddie, what a lovely name. Is this the first murder mystery weekend you've been to?'

'Yes, it is and I know it's going to a lot of fun. And there hasn't been much fun in my life since my dear Robert passed away.' Maddie sighed and then cheered up again. 'You're certainly are out in the sticks here Dickie. I thought the taxi driver was never going to find it. He was getting quite desperate. Still, I'm here now.'

Dickie tried to withdraw his hands which Maddie was still tightly holding onto, 'Come and sit down in the drawing room to recover and I'll rustle up some coffee.'

But Maddie wasn't going to let him out of her sight just yet, 'Why don't you come and sit down as well and tell me all about this weekend.'

No sooner had Dickie manage to open the drawing room door than he was whisked through it.

Chapter 9

Until he ran out of petrol Charles had been congratulating himself on avoiding motorways, which terrified him. One of the reasons he decided to drive down instead of having a lift with Ronald and Marigold was because he knew Ronald would drive down the M4 like a maniac, changing lanes without regard for any other road users.

The other reason was that, in Charles' opinion, Ronald could only aspire to ham acting, but talked as if he had played all the great Shakespearian roles. So, he picked a devious cross-country route which had taken him twice as long as he had anticipated. And then just as he was nearing Kingsford, he hit the gridlock. Stop start motoring soon used up his carefully husbanded petrol and eventually the battered Mini rolled to a stop.

When the drivers behind him realised that continually hooting wasn't going to get it moving again a couple got out and helped him push it off the road and into a gateway.

Grabbing a can from the boot he set off in search of a petrol station. The only thing keeping him from really losing his rag was the fact that he was now going faster than the other cars. Occasionally they would put on a spurt, but a few yards down the road he would overtake them again.

After a while he got to know some of them quite well and they exchanged views on the weather and the best places to go for a cheap holiday.

Strangely none of them offered him a lift, and Charles wondered if this down to the thick horn-rimmed glasses he was wearing. Perhaps they made him look like a psychopath. Although he had no idea what a psychopath looked like. He always wore this pair when playing the part of the Vicar, as they were faintly clerical and definitely comical. He didn't dare take them off as he was as blind as a bat and would probably fall down a drain or into a ditch.

Suddenly, like bath water roaring down the plughole, the traffic roared off and didn't stop. He watched the last tail lights disappearing and realised he was all alone on a country lane with no idea where he was.

He heard a tractor chugging up behind him and stepped onto the grass verge to give it more room. When it had gone past, he saw it was towing his car. 'What the hell?' He ran down the road behind it shouting and waving his arms. Finally, the driver saw him and waited.

'What the devil do you think you're doing with my car?'

'Towing it, like.'

'I can see that, but you've no right to take it.'

'Yes, I 'as, it were blocking up my gateway so I'm taking it back to the farm.'

Uncertain what the country code was for cars left unattended in gateways Charles couldn't think of an immediate answer. But he didn't think the fellow should be allowed to get away with it unchallenged. 'Well, my good man, you'd better not have damaged it.'

'Pay us twenty quid to cover the cost of repairs to the gateway and you'm can have it back.' The driver started to get out of the cab.

The car was no good to Charles and he didn't have twenty quid, but he could just about afford a can of petrol. 'I've run out of fuel. You wouldn't have any would you?'

'I got some derv.'

'Ah.' Charles had no idea what derv was, but didn't want this yokel to think he was ignorant. 'Yes, that'll do. So, if you could just put some in my car, I'm sure we can come to an equitable arrangement.'

'I don't carry it in me cab, it's in the pump at the farm. Hop up and I'll give you a lift.' He leaned across, pushed open the tractor door and pulled down an iron seat next to him. Seeing Charles hesitate, he shouted, 'Look lively lad, I hasn't got all day.'

Charles hauled himself up into the cab in a decidedly un-lively fashion. The iron seat was even more uncomfortable than it looked; and the stench of manure on the farmer's boots made him gag, but before he could jump back down the tractor had lurched forward. A hundred yards along the road the farmer pulled into a farmyard.

While Charles watched he lowered the car, took Charles' can and headed round the side of a dilapidated building. Charles almost stroked the Mini he was so pleased to see looked undamaged. As soon as the derv had been poured into the fuel tank, Charles took out his wallet and removed his last ten-pound note. 'That's all I have.' Then he quickly jumped in the car, started the engine and prepared to make a quick getaway.

The engine started, he put it in gear, but instead of the anticipated fast exit from the farm, the Mini coughed, spluttered, black smoke poured out of the exhaust and it kangaroo hopped across the yard. 'What the hell?' Charles jumped out and stared at his vehicle in horror.

The farmer wandered up to have a look. 'It is a diesel car ain't it.'

'No.'

'Ah, well that's the problem then m'dear, I just put diesel in it.'

'You said it was derv.'

'Same thing ain't it.' And the farmer started to wander off.

Charles looked at the farmer's retreating back and wanted to kill him but that would land him in jail. He bit back the expletives chasing round in his head and said, 'I say, you couldn't help me, could you?'

'Depends what you wants.'

'I'm trying to get to the Vicarage in Kingsford.'

The farmer chewed on a piece of straw. 'Ah, right, the Vicarage.' He chomped more vigorously, pushed back his hat and scratched his head. 'It's a very long way round.' There was more chomping and scratching and a hearty hawk onto the mud. 'Unless you goes cross country like.'

Charles ran three times a week, but on a clean treadmill, in the safe confines of a London gym club, he'd never been across fields with hedges and ditches.

'How far is it…cross country…like?' It wouldn't hurt to adopt the local lingo.

'Bout five miles as the crow flies. Mind you I dunno know why they says that 'cos crows don't never fly straight.'

Charles looked at his fashionable leather shoes which had already given him blisters. Five bloody miles! - he couldn't even run five yards in them.

He looked at the farmer and the farmer looked at him and then said, 'Come on then if you wants this lift.' He jumped back into the cab and waited for Charles to climb in. 'It's gonna get a bit rough going across the fields, they'm not as smooth as the road. So, you'd better hang on tight m'dear.'

With a grinding of gears, they bounced through a gateway and into a muddy field. On the far side of the field the tractor stopped. 'Right, out you gets then and opens that gate.'

Charles looked down at the ground and wanted to die. He slid out of the tractor and saw his feet disappear into what he hoped was mud, but which smelled otherwise. e He untied the twine binding the gate shut and dragged it open.

The tractor drove through spraying him with more mud and waited on the other side. 'Make sure you ties 'im up tight mind, I don't want they bullocks getting out.'

Charles looked up and saw a group of determined animals heading his way at a gallop. He shot up into the cab a lot quicker than he'd got down, and shut the door.

In the next field he not only had to open the gates, but put out some pellets for a flock of vicious-looking sheep which walked all over his feet. And so, the nightmare journey continued across field after field. Sometimes he had to put out food other times he had to count the stupid animals, which wouldn't stand still so he had to start again. None of the gates were easy to open and three fell on his feet and had to be dragged up out of the mud. The farmer sat and shouted instructions or, most of the time, just sat.

Just when he thought he couldn't cope with another gate the tractor shot out of a track and onto a road. Charles had never been so pleased to see tarmac, it was beautiful and smooth, and practically mud-free.

The tractor stopped and the farmer leaned forward on his steering wheel. 'There you are m'dear, all safely delivered.'

'But…where are we?'

'Outside the Vicarage like what you asked for.'

Charles peered through the mud-spattered windscreen and could vaguely make out a large house behind a hedge.

'Out you jump then.'

Charles wasn't sure if he could move, let alone jump out. 'About my car…'

The farmer looked at him for a long moment, chewing vigorously on his bit of straw. 'Tell you what, as you done such a good job giving us a hand, like, I's got a bit of time to spare so bung us your car keys and I'll tow it to the garage for you and get the engine washed through. How does that sound?'

Charles, pathetically grateful, handed them over. 'So, what's your address so that I can come and get it?'

'Church Farm, you can't miss it. It's about a hundred yards down the road there.'

Charles peered where the farmer was pointing and saw the church and then a muddy gateway. He felt slightly sick. The yokel then pointed back up the road behind him. 'And that's where I picked you up.' He'd been virtually outside the Vicarage - all he'd done for the last hour was go round in a big circle, being jolted, trodden on, chased and covered in mud.

'Thank you bloody much,' he muttered after jumping down, aiming a kick at the tractor tire and falling over. The farmer waved and drove off. Charles gingerly tried a few neck exercises to ease the feeling that he had just spent the sixty minutes in a spiteful tumble drier - they didn't help.

He needed to get some dry clothes out of his suitcase, but he couldn't face going along the road to the farm to get it. He'd just been humiliated by a country bumpkin and he wasn't about to risk it again. Besides, he knew Dickie would have brought along his vicar's outfit, he could change into that.

He staggered up the path and banged on the door. It was finally opened by Ronald who'd been sent downstairs by Marigold to grab some more gin bottles.

'Oh, it's you, Charles, making a late entry as usual.'

Charles pushed his way in ready to explode. 'Don't start the minute I walk in the door Ronald, I'm warning you.'

'Oh yes, a bit of eye shadow and a nice red lipstick and I could even fancy you myself. You'll need to have a shower first though you stink to high heaven.'

'You're asking for a good thumping, now get out of my way.'

'I'm only trying to tip you off. Him upstairs has been making a few changes. You'll have to take those glasses off for a start.' Ronald went to snatch at them.

Charles gave him a strong shove, 'Get off I can't see a damn thing without them.'

'We all have to make sacrifices for our craft Charles, and I'm sure you are going to enjoy your new role.'

'What new role?' He grabbed Ronald's shirt and pulled it so they were eyeball to eyeball. 'What are you talking about?'

'Mind my shirt you're getting mud all over it. What the devil have you been doing?'

'To hell with your shirt, what's going on?'

'Oh, that's not very lady-like is it?' Ronald giggled, 'You're going to have a sex change.'

Chapter 10

The noise of their brawling filtered through to Dickie in the drawing room, where he had been listening to Maddie telling him over and over again how excited she was. At least it gave him an excuse to leave. So, promising to come back immediately he burst into the hall and separated them. 'Will you two stop this, the guests have started arriving. And why are you so late Charles?' He stopped and sniffed, 'You stink to high heaven old love.'

'I ran out of petrol - some yokel gave me a lift on his tractor.'

'And what are you doing down here, Ronald? It's not time to mingle yet.'

'I was just going to the loo, old chap.'

'You should have thought of that earlier. Now upstairs, both of you.' He noticed Maddie's suitcase and picked it up. 'Take Mrs Forbes' case up for her, Ronald, she's in the second room along on the left.'

'I'm not the bell boy, I'm the Bishop, let Charles take it.'

Charles stopped trying to wipe the mud off what was left of his shoes. 'What does he mean, he's a bishop? I'm not going anywhere until you tell me about these script changes, Dickie.'

'I have been elevated to higher things, why do you think I'm wearing a purple shirt?' And Ronald smoothed his chest and smirked.

'Because you've got no dress sense.'

Dickie pushed the case into Ronald's hand and pushed them both towards the stairs. 'We don't want the punters to hear all this. We'll talk about it up stairs.' He watched to make certain they had disappeared then opened the door to the drawing room. 'I shan't be long, Maddie. Your case has been taken up, second bedroom on the left. Now if you'll excuse me.'

'I'll be waiting for you Dickie, so don't be long.'

Dickie smiled and quickly shut the door. Then he sprinted up the three flights of stairs to the attic and paused outside the door to get his breath back. Perhaps hiring a whole house wasn't such a good idea; he was going to be exhausted before the weekend was over.

Charles, Ronald and Marigold had obviously been arguing, but they fell silent when he came in. Then they all tried to talk at once.

'Be quiet all of you.' He glared round at them. He still held the whip hand - they'd better toe the line or they wouldn't get paid.

'Right, Charles,' he held up his hand to stop Charles saying a word, 'you are still the Vicar, but…,' he turned and glared at Ronald who was sniggering behind his hand. 'I could always make Charles the Bishop.' He was pleased to see Ronald turn white.

'You wouldn't.'

'I would.' He turned back to Charles. 'You must have read that the good old C of E is now having female vicars, so I thought it would be a good idea to bring our little play up to date and have one ourselves.'

'You can do what you like with your updates, but if you think I'm dressing up as a woman you've got another think coming.'

'Quite right Charles, it's a disgrace.' Marigold clutched his arm to give him moral support – and hurriedly backed off when she caught a whiff of manure. 'Uhhh, your clothes are disgusting.'

'I had a bit of an accident. Dickie, where's my vicar's outfit.'

'There, hanging up by your bed.'

Charles saw a short navy skirt, black tights, navy jumper, a dog collar and a blonde wig. 'I told you I'm not dressing up as a woman, where's what I usually wear?'

'I haven't brought it. And you won't be able to wear those ridiculous glasses either.' Dickie snatched them off Charles' face and then turned to Ronald. 'And you; stop smirking and get into that cope and mitre.'

He looked round for Marigold who had disappeared into her private corner. He heard sounds of slurping. Heaven knows where she'd hidden that bottle, but he didn't have time to take it off her.

'According to that woman this should be the Vicarage.' Freda glared at the building. 'I can't see a name anywhere. Funny sort of hotel that doesn't have a name up.'

74

'That woman didn't seem to think it was a hotel.' Angela thought the woman they had asked directions from in the village knew what she was talking about, but Freda had dismissed her as a local yokel who couldn't understand the Queen's English. And Freda would know of course because she had taught English for many years.

'It's probably fallen down somewhere. Anyway, we're here now so out you get Angela.' Freda marched up to the door, banged on the knocker and stepped back and waited.

Angela stood behind her, wishing they could get back in the car and go home. The gloomy building surrounded by tall trees looked more than a little menacing to her. 'Perhaps there's no one in.'

'Of course there's someone in.' Freda gave the door knocker another almighty bang forcing the door to open slightly. Pushing it back she strode into the hall and looked around. Angela crept in behind her.

'Hello, anyone about?' When this produced no response, Freda banged loudly on the hall table and shouted again. 'Damn fools ought to have someone on reception.'

Angela clutched her coat to her chest. 'Are you sure we've got the right address Freda?'

'Of course I'm sure. Though why your daughter chose such an out of the way place I cannot imagine. Still, it's nothing to do with me. She obviously thought you needed a weekend away.'

'I do need a rest to calm my nerves.' But Angela didn't think Kingsford Vicarage was going to be the place to do that.

'If you spent less time worrying about your nerves, Angela you wouldn't need to calm them so much.'

A sudden horrible thought struck Freda, perhaps her niece hadn't booked them into a country hotel with log fires and good food, but a weekend retreat instead. Angela and her wretched nerves now meant they would have to put up with poor food, long periods of silence interspersed with hymn singing, soul searching and cold rooms.

She was about to tell Angela when Maddie, who'd got tired of waiting for Dickie to come back, decided she really needed that cup of coffee - her appearance from the drawing room, made them both jump.

'Hello ladies, have you just arrived?'

Freda took in the figure-hugging dress, high heels and expensively-cut blonde hair, which had definitely come out of a bottle, and decided this was not the sort of person she expected to be doing a lot of soul-searching. Perhaps it wasn't a retreat after all. 'Yes, we have. I'm surprised there's no one here to greet us.'

'Mr Wilson's around somewhere. Would you like a cup of coffee while you're waiting, I'm just off to find some?'

'Not at the moment no. We'd like to see our room and unpack first.'

Angela would have liked another coffee, but she didn't dare contradict Freda. Instead, she asked if they really were at the Kingsford Hotel.

Maddie looked puzzled. 'Well, it's called Kingsford Vicarage as far as I know. Are you here for the weekend?

'Yes.'

'Then you're in the right place. Right, well, if you'll excuse me, I think I will retreat to the kitchen', Maddie looked around, 'which must be this way.' And she disappeared.

Freda's worst fears were realised so it was a retreat – not only were they in for a weekend of hard beds and boiled cabbage, but it looked as if they were going to have to cook for themselves. She envisioned rotas for making porridge and cleaning the floors.

Angela sighed, 'I wish Barbara wouldn't spring these surprises on me.'

'Yes, well, your daughter's idea of a fun birthday present is a mystery to me too.' But before she could enlighten her sister about what they could expect, Angela was asking if she had remembered to bring some books with her.

Although Angela found life pretty terrifying most of the time, she did enjoy the vicarious thrill of reading about gruesome murders safely contained within the pages of a novel.

Freda glared at her, 'Of course I did; four Agatha Christies and three P D James. And the Horse and Hound for me. But I doubt there will be much time for reading....' Before Freda could complete the sentence,

Dickie rushed down the stairs and seized Angela's hand. 'Hello, are you Mrs Mortimer?'

Angela nodded, unable to take her eyes off his flamboyant waistcoat and bowtie.

Dickie turned to Freda.' And this I take it is the charming Miss Andrews.'

Freda sniffed and kept a firm hold on her handbag to avoid shaking hands. He wasn't her idea of a man leading a retreat.

'Right then ladies, I'm Dickie Wilson. So, welcome to Kingsford Vicarage.'

'And are you the Vicar?' Freda used her best headmistress voice indicating she suspected a lie and would find it out.

'Oh, no, you'll meet him later.' Dickie patted her arm. 'Silly me I keep forgetting, you'll meet her later.'

There was a moment's horrified silence broken only be two deeply indrawn breaths. Angela managed to get out a squeak first. 'A female Vicar! Oh, Freda, we don't hold with them do we.'

Freda's chest expanded like a poulter pigeon. 'Indeed not, Angela.' It was bad enough to be booked in for a retreat, but one led by a woman masquerading as a vicar was not to be born.

'But they're all the rage now, ladies.'

'All the rage!' If Freda had expanded any more, she would have burst. 'They most certainly are not all the rage, not where we come from.'

'You mustn't take it so seriously, it's only a bit of harmless fun.' Dickie moved towards the stairs. 'So, if you'd like to follow me.'

But Freda wasn't budging. 'Harmless fun!' She could hardly get the words out.

While she spluttered Angela added. 'You'll be wanting female bishops next.'

Dickie took her suggestions seriously. 'Now there's a thought.'

This was too much for Freda. 'I'm sorry Angela, but we must cancel our booking immediately.'

Dickie looked from one to the other, 'I'm afraid I won't be able to give you a refund.'

Angela didn't want to fall out with Freda, on the other hand she didn't want to fall out with her daughter either, who could be equally awkward at times. 'Perhaps we had better stay Freda, as Barbara booked it for us. You know, as a present.'

Freda glared at Angela. She wanted to insist they walk straight out, but she hadn't bought any food for the weekend so there was not a lot of point going home. Instead, she turned her icy gaze on Dickie. 'Very well we will stay, but on the understanding that we have as little as possible to do with the said female personage.'

'I'm sure that can be arranged.' Dickie was always magnanimous in victory. 'Now shall I show you to your room?'

But Freda wasn't finished with him yet. 'I think ought to warn you my sister suffers from her nerves, don't you Angela?'

'Always have, always will I'm afraid, Mr Wilson.'

Dickie took Angela's hand and pressed it between his. 'Nothing will happen to make you nervous this weekend, you just relax and enjoy yourselves.'

Angela wasn't used to such kindness and held onto his hand longer than custom dictated. 'We will, and we're really looking forward to our murder mysteries.'

'That's the spirit, Mrs Andrews, you've come to the right place.' He tried to remove his hand. 'Now where's your luggage, I'll take it up for you?'

'Oh, do let go of him Angela.' Freda couldn't stand all this touchy-feely stuff and sincerely hoped there wouldn't be a lot of hugging over the weekend - although she suspected there might be. 'It's still in Master Robin Reliant, we will unload it when we have seen our room.'

'I hope we have one overlooking the garden?' Angela had let go of Dickie's hand and had moved on to clutching his arm.

'They all do. Shall we go up, ladies?' He turned and pointed at the stairs. 'After you.'

Ronald, dressed in his cope and mitre, crept downstairs checking over his shoulder. He'd tiptoed past Dickie who was in one of the bedrooms showing two old biddies round it and from the sounds of it they were less than happy. 'That should keep him out of my hair for a while,' he muttered.

Checking there was no one in the hall he sat down on the bottom step and after a short, but tiring fight with the cope managed to pull a small flask out of his trouser pocket and take a long swig. He'd come down to find the cloak room, but the early morning start plus several swigs up in the attic was making it difficult to keep his eyes open. He leaned against the banisters and started snoring quietly, the mitre slipping further and further down his forehead.

Chapter 11

Now that the guests had started arriving George realised his chances of creeping back to clear Caroline's room unnoticed were very low so he decided to put all his efforts into stopping the Bishop getting to the Vicarage.

As Alan no longer trusted him not to dash back, they were running up and down all the lanes together. Enthusiastically flagging down every red car, they suffered much verbal abuse and, in two cases threats of physical violence.

'It's hopeless,' George was bent over, hands on knees, barely able to speak.

Alan, although younger was not as fit as one would expect of fourth reserve in the village's badminton team. 'Perhaps Miss Jones managed to stop him,' he gasped.

'I don't see how.' George slowly straightened up, and sucked air into his lungs. 'Come on, I'm going back.'

Exhausted they finally returned to the Vicarage fearing the worst. And their worst was realised when they saw a red car parked outside. Somehow it had managed to slip past them.

Alan felt sick. 'It's too late, he's here already.' He wanted to run home, but he had to think of Caroline.

George looked more closely at the car. 'It might be red but it's a Reliant Robin - he wouldn't be driving a three-wheeler surely.'

'Why not, there's no telling what a bishop might do.'

'There's only one way to find out.' George gently pushed open the front door.

The draught of cold air shocked Ronald out of his nap. He jumped up, and from under the mitre saw two men creeping into the hall. Assuming they were two of the guests he quickly hid his flask and assumed his character. He might be an old ham, but he was a professional old ham.

'Ah, good morning my children, um, bless you, bless you.' And he waved his hand in their direction hoping he was giving some kind of benediction.

George and Alan were transfixed in the doorway like rabbits caught in headlights.

'I told you it was his car. Now what do we do?' Alan was the first to find his voice.

But George was first to find his wits. Putting on his most urbane voice he said, 'Good morning, My Lord, we're sorry we missed your arrival.'

'Ah, it matters not, you're here now and I'm sure we're all going to have a thoroughly enjoyable weekend together.'

'You're here for the weekend?' Alan was horrified.

'The whole weekend?' George was even more horrified.

'Oh yes, Saturday and Sunday, we aim to give good value.' Ronald stood up and tried another benedictory wave, but it hurt his head.

'There seems to be a slight misunderstanding My Lord, we thought it was only for the morning.' George's head was starting to hurt as well.

'Oh no, these things usually last the whole weekend. Have you not booked a room?' He wandered over to the table and started leafing through a hymn book while humming 'Onward Christian Soldiers', the only hymn he could remember. Out of the corner of his eye he saw the two men huddled together and judged it was safe to have another swig.

'Now what do we do?' whispered Alan, 'He's obviously expecting to be put up somewhere for the weekend.'

'We stick to the story.' George raised his voice. 'It's about the Vicar, My Lord, there's something you need to know.'

'Oh yes, what's he done?' Ronald tried not to laugh but couldn't help himself. 'Sorry, sorry, I was forgetting there's been a few changes round here. So, what's she done?

'This is a rather embarrassing, My Lord, but the Vicar's had a little operation, and what with one thing and another quite forgot to mention it.'

'Really, what sort of operation?' Ronald was all ears.

'It's a bit delicate, My Lord.'

'Yes, but there won't be any more children,' and then to make certain that the Bishop was under no misapprehensions Alan added, 'Not that there were any mistakes to start with. That was all a misunderstanding by Miss Jones.'

'Ohhhh, that sort of operation.' Ronald's giggles ended in an attack of hiccups.

'Obviously this is between ourselves My Lord.' George thought the Bishop was taking the news better than expected.

'Absolutely, Mum's the word, dear boy.'

'Most understanding of you, My Lord.'

'I can't wait to go and tell her ladyship. It might even put her off her gin.'

'I'm not sure you ought to…,'

'The Bishop knows best, Alan, so if he wants to dash off home and tell his wife we mustn't hold him up.' George opened the front door. 'So, I expect you'd like to leave straight away, My Lord.' He even gave a slight bow.

'I'd love to, dear boy, but I'm not allowed, well not until Sunday afternoon anyway.'

George's headache became a whole lot worse. 'But you can't stay here.'

'Oh yes, I must, or I won't get paid.'

'Paid?'

'Yes, we get special weekend rates with overtime on Sundays.'

Alan muttered to himself, 'No wonder they volunteer for all those services.'

Ronald went into acting overdrive and rolled his eyes heavenwards and up the stairs. 'Not that that him upstairs pays much, but I need the money. A little debt to be settled - you know. An affair of the heart.'

George and Alan looked at each other in disbelief. George recovered first. 'Perhaps you could spend the weekend with Mr Palmer here.'

'What!' Alan glared at George who ignored him.

'Yes, he would be delighted if you stayed with him, wouldn't you Alan?'

'George, could I have a word with you?' Alan most definitely wasn't delighted.

'Well, that's very civil of you dear boy,' Ronald patted Alan's arm, 'very civil indeed.' He leaned in closer. 'To be frank I'm not overly keen on the attic.'

Alan, almost overcome by Ronald's whisky breath, managed to squeak, 'The attic? What were you doing in the attic?'

'It's unbelievable isn't it? I shouldn't be telling you this of course, but all is not as it should be.' Ronald rolled his eyes up the stairs again. 'Him, upstairs, has been making changes.'

'Changes. What sort of changes?' George's urbane manner had long since disappeared.

'I used to be the Honourable Giles Forsythe.' Seeing their sceptical looks he added, 'Yes, really.'

'What, before you before you became a bishop?'

'To think I've sunk as low as this.' Ronald was now in full luvvie mode. 'I've trodden the boards at Stratford you know. Ah the immortal Bard.' He hunched his back and limped round the hall. 'Now is the winter of our discontent made glorious summer by this sun of York.'

When he had his back to them, he took another quick slurp from the flask then turned and grabbed George by the lapels and pulled him in close, noses practically touching. 'But I have been passed over, thrown out on the scrap heap of rancid grease paint. It makes me so angry.'

Now George turned his head, trying to avoid the whisky fumes. 'Please try to calm down My Lord.'

Ronald pushed him away. 'You're quite right, I must be calm. If only I could have a little drink.'

'I think he's already had a little drink,' Alan whispered.

George agreed with him, but needed to take charge of the situation. 'Right, I'm sure Mr Palmer can find you something at his house. Shall we go?' He opened the front door.

Alan immediately closed it. 'He can't stay with me for the weekend.'

'Is there a problem dear boy? I won't take up much room, and I shall be taking all my meals here of course, it's all part of my duties.'

'I'm sure it can all be sorted out at Mr Palmer's.' George opened the front door.

Alan closed it. 'George, you are not listening to me, we've only got two bedrooms, mother's and mine, there is nowhere for the Bishop to sleep.'

'Oh, come dear boy, please don't disappoint me now.' Ronald gave him his most pleading look.

At that moment, Maddie wandered across the hall holding a mug of coffee. She'd found the kitchen deserted and after a walk round the garden had put the kettle on and made herself some instant. 'Oh, you two are back and with a bishop.'

Ronald beamed at her, 'And you are dear lady?'

'Madeleine Forbes, your Grace.'

George quickly improvised. 'One of our Lay Readers My Lord.'

'Ah, a lay reader,' Ronald leered at Maddie, 'On second thoughts, I think I'll stay here.'

'No really, My Lord, I think you ought to come with us, didn't he Alan?'

'No, absolutely not George.'

'And Mr Palmer has got some nice malt whisky at home, haven't you?'

Ronald was torn. Malt whisky or perhaps a lay down with a lay reader? No reason why he couldn't have both, but the whisky first. 'Ah well, now you're talking my language, old chap,' He smiled at Maddie. 'Sorry, dear lady, I have to go now, but I'll be back.'

Maddie smiled back and headed up the stairs. 'I'll see you later then Bishop.'

'You certainly will dear lady, you certainly will.' He draped himself over the banisters and waved fondly at her, all thoughts of Dickie's ban on seducing the guests completely forgotten. 'Bye, bye. Tata.' And he blew her a kiss.

George watched until Maddie disappeared then said, 'Come on, Alan, we'd better get him moving.'

'I told you, I don't have anywhere to put him.'

'He can sleep in the bath. Keep giving him whisky and he won't notice.'

'No, but mother will, we've only got one bathroom.'

'You sleep in the bath then.'

'Why can't he stay with you, George?'

'Oh, stop being so selfish and think of Caroline for a change.'

Ronald was still staring up the stairs. 'Charming woman, charming. I've been told to keep my hands off the women this weekend, but just one won't hurt surely.' He swung round the newel post and leered at them.

'Did you hear that, George?'

'I'm sure your mother will be safe.'

'But what about the dog?'

'It's a Pekinese, he'll probably think it's a toilet brush. Just keep him until Sunday afternoon and then Caroline will be back.'

'But…,'

'Look, it's obvious he doesn't want to see Caroline straight away.'

'But…,'

George gave Alan a nudge in the ribs. 'And she'll be full of gratitude for the way you handled the situation. How you kept the Bishop happy until she came back.'

'But…,'

'You'll be her little hero, won't you?' This was followed by another nudge plus a wink.

'If I take the Bishop you have got to cancel this murder mystery weekend.'

'Don't worry about that now.'

'George, promise me.'

Ronald undraped himself from the post. 'Well lead on, dear boy, lead on.' He pulled himself up and brandished an imaginary sword. 'Once more into the

breach, dear friends. Friends, Romans and Countrymen.'
This was followed by two loud burps and a rendition of
'When you've got Friends and Neighbours'. Finally,
overcome with emotion he slid down to the floor and
closed his eyes.

George and Alan stared at him and then at each other.
Alan had a vision of his mother's face when she saw the
Bishop the worse for wear. George had a vision of his
wife's face if he didn't pay the caterers. 'We'd better try
and get him on his feet.'

Between them they managed to get Ronald into a
standing position and he immediately put his arms round
George's neck and looked deeply into his eyes. 'It was
him upstairs who made me become a bishop you know.'

'You were called were you, My Lord?'

Ronald waved a finger. 'No, he didn't have the
courtesy to phone. It was revealed to me out of the blue.'

'Like on the road to Damascus?' Alan thought he
should at least try to sound like a Church Warden who
knew his bible.

Ronald tried to focus and stared blearily out of the
window. 'This is Damascus is it? Funny, I could have
sworn the signpost said Kingsford. I'd better get my eyes
tested.'

'You can do that on Monday My Lord, shall we go?'
George and Alan tried to manoeuvre him to the front
door, but Ronald was in no hurry.

He sighed tragically and gazed at Alan. 'She said I
was a has-been and she's going to have a younger lover.'

'What? Who?'

'Marigold.'

'Marigold! That sounds like the name of a cow.'

'You're so right dear boy, that's just what she...,'

George had heard enough. 'Should you be telling us all this?'

'No, but I had to tell someone.' He turned and tried to focus on George. 'And you've got such understanding eyes.'

'Has he?' Alan had known George for more than twenty years and had never thought George was understanding about anything.

Ronald turned back to Alan, 'I'd seen the signs of course.'

'Signs! what signs?'

'The snide remarks about my abilities.'

'Do you think he's hallucinating, George?'

'I think he's off his rocker.' George made another attempt to move Ronald nearer the front door. 'Come along My Lord, this way.'

'I wonder if he's left anything behind. Didn't he say he'd been up in the attic?'

'What you mean his crook or something?' George pushed Ronald into Alan's arms. 'You carry on I'll go and check.' And leaving Alan struggling to keep Ronald upright he nipped up the stairs.

Ronald put his arms round Alan's neck, giving him the full benefit of his whisky breath again when the mitre slipped down over his eyes. 'I say old chap, I think I've gone blind.'

'Blind drunk more like.' Alan pushed the mitre back up.

'That's a miracle, an absolute miracle. I was blind and now I can see.'

'Can you see the front door?'

'Yes, yes, it's over there.' Ronald pointed vaguely in front him.

'Well, let's try and get through it shall we?'

'Lead on dear boy, I'm right behind you.'

'In front might be safer,' and Alan pushed him none too gently through the door and down the path.

Once outside he decided the easiest way to get the Bishop back to his house was to drive him there. He tried the door to the Reliant Robin but it was locked. 'Could I have the key, sir?'

Ronald peered at the three-wheeler. 'That little toy isn't my car.'

Alan scowled; George was right when he said the Bishop wouldn't be driving a Reliant. He looked round for another red car, but couldn't see one. 'So where are you parked, sir?'

Ronald swayed precariously. 'I've no idea. Somewhere round here.'

'Give me your keys and I'll see if I can find it.'

Ronald fumbled under his cope. 'Sorry old boy, they're in the attic.'

Alan wanted to scream. What had possessed the Bishop to leave his car keys in the attic? 'What are they doing up there, sir?'

'Cause I left them in my jacket pocket.' Ronald gave Alan a look which suggested what he'd done was completely normal.

Alan looked around for help. He couldn't leave the Bishop lurching about in front of the Vicarage while he went upstairs and got them and he could hardly tie him up to stop him wandering off. 'I'm afraid we will have to walk then, sir.' And putting his arm round Ronald's waist he attempted to steer him down the road.

Their progress was punctuated by several stops while Ronald told Alan how wonderful he was. When they reached the High Street, Alan kept his fingers crossed that they wouldn't meet anyone, but his digits failed him. Still standing outside the Post Office was the same group of people who were there earlier in the morning.

As there was very little excitement in Kingsford, villagers tended to spend much of their time outside the Post Office on the off chance that one day there would be something worth watching. And this morning their patience was rewarded. A hum ran round the gathering, 'It's the Bishop,' and they rushed forward for a closer look.

Alan tried to steer Ronald past them, but an actor of Ronald's calibre wasn't going to pass up on an audience. 'Good morning dear people, good morning,' and he doffed his mitre.

Several came up and asked Ronald to bless them which he obligingly did with many flourishes - and kisses for the best-looking ladies. The enterprising owner of the post office, seeing more villagers than usual, quickly put some tables and chairs outside in the sun and started serving coffee and cakes.

Alan finally managed to tear Ronald away from the group, which had now swelled to two dozen, and he was keenly aware that they were all watching with interest his struggle to get Ronald down the road.

As they neared his house, Alan's stomach churned even more. He might get away with persuading his mother to allow the Bishop to stay, but not one in this state. She was strictly teetotal apart from a small sherry after church on Sunday.

He considered walking Ronald up and down until he sobered up, but how long would that take? And besides the man was heavy and Alan was tired of holding him up. Although he noticed Ronald was able to support himself while giving the blessings. Probably a thing Bishops were taught to do.

He paused when they reached the little bridge spanning the stream. It wasn't very wide and would require careful negotiating. He knew in his heart that Ronald would fall in and his heart wasn't wrong. After some serious swaying and some un-bishop-like cursing Ronald slipped off the edge and into the water.

His outraged yelp was prompted by the coldness of the water rather than the depth because it only came halfway up his calf. Alan guided him to the bank and pulled him out. His mother was going to be even less impressed by a drunken bishop, who dripped water all over her carpets.

Alan opened the front door and cautiously called out, 'Mother.' Nothing. He left Ronald clinging to the doorpost and went into the kitchen. For the first, and the last, time that day Alan had a stroke of luck. On the kitchen table was a note saying she had gone out with her cousin who had called unexpectedly.

But she hadn't taken Ping with her, and the Pekinese rushed up to Ronald, sniffed his trousers, which smelt of water weed and duck poo, and lifted his leg. Fortunately, Ronald didn't notice the additional liquid and attempted to pat the little dog on the head before blessing him.

Alan finally managed to manhandle Ronald into the bathroom, promised him a dry pair of trousers, got him a bottle of whisky, and then locked him in. Ping settled down outside the door growling and barking as he saw fit - he had never felt so brave.

All Alan wanted to do was collapse in a chair and forget all about what was happening at the Vicarage. But a picture of Caroline kept floating before his eyes. He hoped she would appreciate his efforts to stop the Bishop finding out she had forgotten about his visit. He closed his eyes and in his little daydream she called him her hero.

However, there was still the murder mystery weekend to stop. He didn't trust George to cancel it so it was down to him. And where the hell was George? He should be here helping with the Bishop.

Alan scowled George was probably relaxing somewhere, having a cup of coffee.

Chapter 12

'Get out of here at once, you filthy pervert.' George quickly slammed the attic door, his heart racing. He turned and ran down the stairs, but he couldn't rid himself of the sight of a semi-naked Marigold screaming at him.

Once he'd got rid of Alan and the Bishop, he'd raced up stairs to check that Herbert hadn't left anything behind. Then he was going to empty Caroline's room, but he was too late. As he ran along the landing, he saw Dickie and two women coming out of it.

'Ah George, let me introduce you to two of our guests, Mrs Mortimer and Miss Andrews.'

'If I could just have a quick word.'

'In a minute George,' Dickie turned to the sisters, 'I'm sure you'll find this bedroom equally spacious and it is right next door to the bathroom.' And he opened the next door along on the landing. 'Now, would you like me to fetch your luggage?'

Freda peered into the room, gave it a quick glare and decided it was acceptable, 'We are perfectly capable of getting our own luggage. Come along Angela.'

Dickie waited until they had disappeared into the room and then glared at George, 'What's going on? Those two were booked into the room with the *ensuite* but when I took them in there it was in use. I've had to move them to another room and give them a discount.'

'Ah, yes…there was someone staying here for a few days and the cleaners must have forgotten to do that room. I hope that doesn't affect my money.'

'Not as long as you get it sorted out it out otherwise there won't be enough rooms for all my guests - and then that will affect what I'm paying you.'

George's stomach felt hollow, time was ticking away and he needed to pay the deposit. 'I'll sort out the room in a minute, but if you could just pay me first, I need to…pay it into the bank.'

'I'm sure you do old love and once you have fulfilled your side of our agreement you can toddle off. By the way what were you doing in the attic?'

'Ah, just checking everything was alright.'

'I bet you got a flea in your ear. Marigold is not in the best of moods so don't go upsetting her.'

'I wouldn't dream of it.' George thought if anyone was upset over the encounter it was him. 'So as soon as I've done the bedroom, you'll pay me.' He rushed to the airing cupboard and flung back the door, a pile of towels fell out and tried to trip him up.

Dickie watched him frantically struggling to pull out some sheets, sending even more linen onto the carpet. 'No, I'll pay you when I see the caterers. Until they arrive you haven't kept to your side of the bargain. Perhaps you ought to phone them, see what's happening.'

As George grappled with a duvet cover, he heard an unusual ringing sound and saw Dickie take a mobile phone out of his pocket. He felt a stab of envy, he'd wanted one for ages, but couldn't justify the expense, but after this weekend, well, who knows.

Dickie clamped it to his ear. 'Hello, old love, where are you...what? You can't do this to me...hello, hello.' He closed the mobile phone and glared at George. 'The scumbags, I'll sue them for this.'

'What's happened?'

'What's happened, I'll tell you what's happened, half my cast have decided to take another job that's what's happened.' He paced up and down the landing.

'Is that a major problem?'

'No, it's not a major problem,' he paced faster, 'it's a total disaster. I shall have to cancel the whole weekend.'

This was the best bit of news George had had all morning - as long as he got his money of course. He started shoving towels, sheets and duvet covers back into the cupboard.

Dickie quickly put him right on that score. 'Of course, there won't be any money for the church roof fund.'

'What! You can't do that.'

'I will have to give all the guests their money back and I will still have to pay Marigold, Ronald and Charles.'

'There must be something you can do. Just use the actors you've got.'

Dickie started pacing again. 'Great, one of them can murder themselves and then come back to life to help solve the mystery. Yes, very authentic.'

'Can't you find someone else?'

'At this short notice, of course I can't, they'd never get here in time.' His pacing became more agitated, reminding George of Groucho Marx. 'I mean I could take one of the roles at a pinch, but I still need two more people.' He stopped and looked at George. 'There might be a way.'

George could feel himself relaxing slightly. The bank notes which had been receding were starting to come back into view. 'That's good.'

'Can you read?'

'Of course I can.'

'Problem solved.' Dickie beamed. 'You can take one of the parts and your sidekick, Alan can take the other.'

'Oh no, hang on a minute.'

'You want the money - you take the part.'

George now started pacing the landing. This was madness, and Alan would never agree it. On the other hand, he needed the cash. 'What would we have to do?'

'Well, Charles will have to take over Angus's role as the Hon Giles Forsythe as that's a major part and I can be Lydia, Alicia's maid. So, you can choose between being Lady Alicia's Butler or the Vicar.'

'Well, a vicar shouldn't be too difficult.'

'Lovely. I'll go and get the falsies and the wig.'

'Are you mad? I'm not dressing up as a woman.'

'You won't be a woman; you'll be a lady vicar.'

George didn't see that would make any difference, 'No absolutely not.'

'Okay, Alan will have to do it then.'

George allowed himself a brief picture of Alan in drag, 'Oh yes, no problem, he'll love it.' As the picture faded, reality kicked in and he wondered how he could blackmail Alan into doing it.

During his short reverie Dickie had headed down stairs muttering something about Ronald.

George rushed down after him, 'So, if I'm the butler what will I have to do?'

'Not much, just wait on Lady Alicia.'

At that moment the front door opened and Angela and Freda came back carrying their overnight bags and wearing rain coats. The weather, like George's mood, had taken a turn for the worse and a small cloud was emptying itself over the Vicarage.

While unloading the car, Freda explained to Angela that she wasn't having a birthday treat, quite the opposite. Then the heavens had opened making the weekend even more dismal. To help them get through the ordeal they agreed to ignore what was going on, to speak to no one unless it was absolutely necessary and to stay in their room as much as possible.

So disregarding Dickie and George, Freda looked round the hall for a suitable place to hang their wet coats. 'As there doesn't appear to be any hooks we will leave them here Angela.' And, carefully draping them over the newel post, they picked up their bags.

Dickie turned to George. 'Ah George, would you carry those bags up for the ladies?'

'What?'

Dickie hissed, 'That's also one of your duties…as the butler.'

George reluctantly went to take the bags, but Freda raised an imperious hand. 'We will carry our own luggage thank you.' And they swept up the stairs.

George waited until they'd disappeared and then said, 'I wouldn't have to sleep here, would I?'

'No, I suppose not, as long you and Alan come in early tomorrow. But you will have to stay the rest of today and tomorrow to act out the little scenes for the punters. I've got the scripts upstairs.

'I don't get murdered, do I?'

'No, it's Giles who gets shot; he's bumped off by the Vicar, using the gun. Have you still got it by the way?'

George felt down his trousers; he'd got so used to having the gun there he'd forgotten all about it. He pulled it out and gave it to Dickie.

'No hang on to it.'

'Why, I don't need it?'

'No, but Alan will so give it to him.'

George reluctantly put the gun back in his pocket. How the hell was he going to get Alan to shoot someone? 'So where does all this take place?'

'In the drawing room; the body is found by the Bishop when he goes in there after dinner.'

'Oh, there's a bishop as well?'

'Yes, Ronald Harvey's taking the part. He's been wondering around in his cope and mitre practising, but I want him back upstairs.

George was seized with a sudden dread. 'A cope and mitre?'

'He's an old ham, but I have to say he really looks the part. Only problem is he likes a tipple, know what I mean.'

George suddenly felt very queasy – surely they hadn't…but he didn't dare finish the thought.

'Hello again darlings.'

George pulled his hands away from his face and saw Maddie coming down the stairs with her coffee cup.

'Ah, Maddie, I see one of the staff has made you some coffee.' Dickie took the cup from her.

'No, you dear sweet man, I made it myself. I hope that was all right.' And taking the cup back, added, 'I'll just go and wash it up.'

Dickie took it and gave it to George. 'No, no, let George do it, that's what butlers are for.'

Maddie switched her attentions to George, who was still glaring at Dickie, 'You didn't tell me earlier that you're the butler. But will you be the one to do it?'

'What, wash your cup?'

'No, the murder, it's always the butler who does it. Or are you bluffing? You have a very cheeky look in your eye.'

George thought it was more likely to be terror. 'No, it's probably just a bit of fluff.'

'Why don't we both go and do the washing up.' Maddie took George's arm in a firm grip and pulled him towards the kitchen.

Dickie called after them, 'And while you two are doing that I'm going to look for Bishop Ronald, he's probably holed up in the cloakroom.'

Chapter 13

Charles tottered down stairs in a pair of four-inch-high heels. The navy skirt was very tight and very short, the tights were cutting into his crotch and the long blond wig was hot and itchy.

He'd been adamant that he wasn't going to wear the outfit, but his own clothes were so wet and muddy he thought he would come down with pneumonia if he didn't get them off. Marigold, in a rare show of domesticity, had offered to wash them and they were now soaking in the wash basin in the bathroom.

To add to the ignominy while he was putting on the skirt, Dickie gone off with his glasses and threatened to dock his pay if he didn't wear the wig. He needed to get his luggage, but that meant going to farm and he wasn't sure he could face that at the moment.

'Dickie, where are you? I am going to kill you for this.' Groping his way round the hall walls for support he found his way into the library.

Herbert's confidence was severely dented when after several detours he still got caught up in the jam, so he wasn't in the best frame of mind when he finally arrived at the Vicarage much later than he intended. His thermos had long been emptied and the effect of too much caffeine on his dodgy ticker had pushed his blood pressure sky high.

After tucking the Rover in the far corner of the drive so his wife wouldn't see it, if she should happen to go past, he stomped up the steps to the Vicarage and banged on the front door. To his surprise it opened. Muttering under his breath that anyone could have walked in, he walked in himself.

Unbeknown to Bishop Herbert, he bore a strong similarity to Ronald. Both were tall and grey-haired with aquiline features and a tendency towards crankiness.

The likeness was certainly enough to fool the myopic Charles, who staggered back out of the library. He squinted at the figure in the purple shirt and said, 'What are you staring at?'

Herbert was sure Caroline hadn't looked quite so butch before, but he quickly recovered his composure and said, 'Ah the good lady herself; I'm so pleased to meet you again, my dear.' And to get a better look he took off his glasses to give them a good clean.

Which was unfortunate as Charles gave him a hard shove as he walked past, knocking them to the floor and muttering, 'Give it a rest you old soak. Just leave me alone.'

Herbert could hardly believe his ears. 'Kindly address your Bishop with due respect young lady.' In fact, he was so shocked he couldn't even pick up his glasses.

'Don't push your luck, mate.' Charles headed towards the stairs and shouted, 'Dickie, if you think I'm going to keep these clothes on the whole weekend you've got another think coming.'

If he was shocked before the Bishop was now incandescent. 'I beg your pardon!'

'Oh, bog off.'

'Bog off? Really I must insist you speak to me in the proper manner.'

Charles turned and glared at him before heading towards the kitchen, 'That's it, I'm taking them off.' He started to unbutton his skirt and trod on Herbert's glasses as the same time

Herbert grabbed his arm, 'Great heavens! Stop this unseemly conduct at once.'

'Right, you've asked for it, Ronald.' Charles pulled himself free, flailed wildly in the general direction of his target and more by luck than intention caught Herbert fairly and squarely in the right eye.

The effect was startling. Herbert staggered backwards across the hall at the same time that Charles' skirt fell down. Luckily Maddie and George were coming out of the kitchen and the latter was just in time to catch the unfortunate Bishop before he hit the ground.

Hearing the commotion Dickie rushed out of the cloakroom where he had availed himself of the facilities when it was clear that Ronald wasn't in there.

The same commotion also caused Freda and Angela to break their determination to stay in their room and come to the top of the stairs. They stared in amazement at seeing so many people in the hall, all at one time.

Everyone stared at Charles with his skirt round his ankles and then at the unconscious Herbert lying in George's arms.

Dickie was the first to recover. He rushed over to Charles, treading on Herbert's glasses on the way for good measure. 'For crying out loud, what did you do that for?'

'He's been asking for it ever since I got here. Swanking about just because he's the bishop.'

Angela and Freda had been holding their breath for so long they had both gone purple, but finally Angela managed to gasp, 'Freda, did you see that?'

'I said no good would come from the ordination of women.'

'Yes, you did Freda, and I agreed with you.'

Maddie clapped her hands. 'Well done everyone I never realised it would all look so realistic. You've even broken his glasses.'

Charles kicked the shattered spectacles across the floor. 'It'll serve him right if I've broken his nose.'

Dickie, realising the guests were watching, tried to rescue the situation. 'Now Vicar, that's no way to behave to the Bishop.' He then hissed in Charles ear, 'Watch it.'

But there was no way Charles was going to 'watch it'. As far as he could see the weekend was turning into one disaster after another. 'Bollocks to the Bishop, he's just a nasty piece of work.'

Angela, as much to her surprise as Charles, ran down the stairs and gave him a hearty kick on the shins. 'Oh, you wicked woman you, take that.'

'Owww that hurt, what did you do that for, you daft old biddy?'

Freda, not to be outdone ran down as well. 'Don't speak to my sister like that young woman,' and gave him a hefty kick on the other shin.

Everyone then started shouting at each other until Marigold appeared at the top of the stairs clutching a bottle of gin. Using the full force of her powerful voice she screamed, 'Can't you keep the noise down, I've got a headache.'

Dickie glared at her, 'I told you to keep off the alcohol.'

'I wouldn't need alcohol if you didn't keep me in the attic, Dickie. And I'm telling you I'm as mad as hell about it.'

Angela clutched her sister. 'Freda, he's got a mad woman in the attic! I know we said we'd stay, but I can't cope with a mad woman in the attic.'

'Don't worry Angela, we are leaving.' She glared round the hall. 'And don't anyone try to stop us.'

And nobody did so they were able to make it through the front door unscathed. Luckily the sun was once again beaming down on the Vicarage.

When the door closed behind them Maddie clapped her hands again. 'Wow, this is so exciting.'

'I am going to have a bath.' Marigold turned dramatically and disappeared.

George was finding Herbert rather heavy and lowered him to the ground. 'Will someone tell me what's going on? Is this one of your actors Dickie?'

Charles sneered. 'Actor! Ronald! That's a laugh.'

Dickie peered at the unconscious body. Then he looked at Charles. 'What the hell have you done? This isn't Ronald.'

'Of course, it is.'

'It isn't, Ronald doesn't wear glasses,' and Dickie kicked the mangled frames across the floor towards him, 'he should but he doesn't.' He bent over and pulled Herbert's head up for Charles to have a good look.'

Charles got up close and squinted at it. 'Bloody hell. So, who is it, one of the guests?'

'I don't think so, not dressed like this. Is he someone you know George?'

George turned white and his knees buckled. 'Oh my God, this must be Bishop Herbert.'

Chapter 14

Freda quickly realised that storming out in high dudgeon only works if you have somewhere to go. They were now outside the Vicarage while their clothes and the car keys were inside.

Angela, who was still on a high after kicking one of the dreaded female vicars, suggested they go for a walk round the village and look for somewhere to have a cup of tea.

'Don't be ridiculous Angela, we will wait ten minutes for those dreadful people to go away and then we will collect our things and leave.'

In the hall, chaos still reigned. George and Maddie were fighting over the unconscious Herbert. While George was patting his face to revive him Maddie was trying to give him the kiss of life. Having done a first aid badge in the Girl Guides she was always ready to render help.

'Madam, please, he's still breathing.' George then tried to stop her removing Herbert's jacket.

Dickie grabbed George's arm and pulled him away. 'Did you say he was Bishop Herbert? What's he doing here? He's not on my list of guests.'

'Did I say Bishop Herbert?' George lowered his voice, 'Ah…sorry just a slip of the tongue. No, that's…Herbert Bishop…one of our local farmers. He must have just wandered in.' He glanced across and saw Maddie enthusiastically pumping up and down on the Bishop's chest in time to 'Nellie the Elephant'.

He tried to go across to stop her but Dickie held onto him. 'Wandered in! We can't have the locals just wandering.'

George was about to say he'd deal with it when he heard Maddie say, 'He feels very cold; I think he ought to be in bed.'

George swung round to see her trying to lift Herbert into a sitting position and shouted, 'Put him down, Madam.'

'Yes, you don't know where he's been.' Charles had checked to see if he was the farmer who'd given him a lift, but he wasn't. However, his recent experiences had made him nervous of getting too close to anyone involved in agriculture.

'But why's he dressed like a bishop?' Dickie didn't want two bishops wandering around and messing up his play.

'Ah...the Common Agricultural Policy, weevils in his Y-fronts, the usual problems.'

'Why would that make him dress up?'

George, who was now hanging onto Herbert to stop Maddie from pulling him towards the stairs, said, 'It's the stress, it's sent him over the edge. But don't worry Dickie, I'll take him home, it won't take me long.'

'You can't go off now, remember what we agreed earlier, I need you here.'

'Yes, but...'

111

Dickie hissed, 'I take it you want your money.' Then in a louder voice 'We'll keep him here for now and try to sort something out when he comes round.'

Maddie immediately started tugging again. 'Leave him with me, I'll look after him.'

Dickie gave her a relieved smile. 'How kind, Maddie, a regular little Florence Nightingale aren't you.'

George's attempt to intervene was cut off by Dickie continuing, 'And as soon as he's on his feet we'll slip him a couple of quid and he can wander off home again.'

Dickie then turned to Charles. 'Right, perhaps the Reverend Thorn would like to put her skirt back on and help move him.'

'Me! Why me?'

'Because I say so. Where did do you want him, Maddie?'

Maddie smiled at Dickie. 'Put him in my room.'

'No, you can't…'

'Don't worry so much, George, it's the safest place for him.'

'You must be joking.'

Dickie glared at Charles. 'Of you go then, Vicar.'

George had one last attempt to save Herbert. 'I don't think the Vicar will be able to carry him on her own. I'll give her a hand.' He struggled to pick Herbert up, but couldn't.

Dickie patted his arm. 'I think you'll find the Reverend Thorn will be able to manage.'

They all watched while Charles, who also lifted weights as well as running at his gym, effortlessly pick up the unconscious bishop.

'See, what did I tell you George, the Vicar can carry him.'

Charles turned and glared at Dickie. 'I still want a word with you, Dickie.' Then he started walking up the stairs.

Maddie could hardly believe her eyes. 'My word, you are a big strong girl. It's the second on the left.' And she rushed after him.

George tried to follow. 'I really think I ought to go with him.'

'It's all right George; she'll have him in bed in a minute. With a bit of luck, he won't know what's hit him.'

George gazed up the now empty stairs. 'That's what's worrying me.'

Freda looked at her watch; the allotted ten minutes had passed. She pushed open the front door and followed by the still excited Angela entered the hall where they were welcomed with open arms by Dickie.

'Ah Mrs Mortimer, Miss Andrews, come in, come in, I'm so sorry about that, just a slight misunderstanding, but it's all sorted out now.

Angela, who secretly would have liked to have had another go at kicking the vicar, had to make do with hissing, 'A slight misunderstanding! I think it was more than that.'

Freda, who was surprised at Angela's outburst quickly added, 'We witnessed fighting, swearing, drunkenness…,'

Before she could continue Angela had once again jumped in, 'And insanity, don't forget the insanity, Freda.'

Freda needed to get things back to the status quo where she was the sister in charge. 'Poor Angela's nerves are shot to pieces Mr Wilson.'

Angela's nerves were better than they'd been for a long time, but her little rebellion against Freda's authority quickly subsided and she merely nodded in agreement.

George seeing Dickie was distracted tried to edge towards the stairs again. 'He ought to have someone he knows with him when he comes round.'

Without taking his eyes off Freda, Dickie's arm shot out and held George in a vice-like grip. 'A nice cup of coffee will soon put you right Mrs Mortimer. George, a tray of coffee in the drawing room please.'

Before Angela could say that would be lovely, Freda said, 'I'm sorry Mr Wilson, but the offer of a cup of coffee is not going to compensate for that disgraceful episode just now.'

'Something stronger then, what about some gin? I have some in the dining room.'

'Oh, we never touch alcoholic beverages, do we Freda.'

'We most certainly do not. Kindly fetch our suitcases and we will go.'

114

Dickie couldn't afford to lose any guests. 'Now, now, come along Miss Andrews, you're here now and you're unpacked so why not stay? Hmmm?'

Freda was having none of it. 'If you won't get them then I will.'

George, hoping to take advantage of Dickie's attempt to schmooze Freda said, 'No, I'm the butler, I'll go and get them.' But the vice-like grip tightened again.

'No, I need you down here.' Dickie turned to Freda, 'What if I was to offer you another small refund to make up for Mrs Mortimer's nerves. How does that sound eh?'

Angela thought it sounded good, but needed to know that Freda agreed. 'What do you think Freda?'

'I suppose we could give it one more try - on the understanding that nothing more untoward happens this weekend.'

'That's the spirit, ladies. Right, George, coffee for Miss Andrews and Mrs. Mortimer.'

Freda gave George a long hard stare. 'I suppose you are a proper butler - you're not dressed like one?'

'George is highly experienced, but he is new to Lady Alicia's establishment and hasn't had time to change into his uniform.'

Angela couldn't believe her ears. 'Lady Alicia? Oh, Freda, we've never stayed anywhere with a titled lady before. Will I have to curtsey?'

'Don't be ridiculous Angela.'

'No, no, we don't stand on ceremony here, ladies.'

But Angela wanted ceremony. 'So, you're Lady Alicia's butler. Oh, my goodness,' and she almost curtseyed to George.

'Yes, and as Lady Alicia's butler I'll just go upstairs and see how she's getting on.'

'No need George, she'll be in the bath by now.'

'Good, I'll scrub her back then.' And with one last wrench he was free and up the stairs.

Freda glared after him. 'Do butlers usually do that sort of thing?'

Dickie sighed. 'Apparently so.'

Angela was now on the hunt for more eminent guests. 'And is the Bishop staying here as well Mr Wilson?' She hoped he was because she intended telling him how she'd kicked the vicar who had knocked him out.

'Oh, he wasn't a real bishop you know, just some local farmer who likes to dress up.'

'As a bishop?' Freda's antenna twitched.

'Don't worry, he'll be gone soon Miss Andrews.'

'Supposing he comes back, it might not be safe.'

'No, no, he's quite harmless, so if you see him again just push him out the front door and send him home. Right, I'll go and get your coffee; you go and sit in the drawing room.'

As soon as Dickie had disappeared to the kitchen Angela couldn't contain her excitement. 'Fancy a Lady staying here, Freda, I expect that's why Barbara chose it for us.'

116

Freda gave one of her famous sniffs. 'Titled ladies or not, I'm having serious doubts this so-called retreat. In fact, we are going to write to the Archbishop about it.'

'Can we have coffee first, Freda?'

'If we must.'

George hammered on Maddie's door. 'Maddie, please, you have to let me in.'

The door opened a fraction and Maddie's head appeared round it. 'Oh, it's you. Well, I'm sorry my sweet, but I'm a bit busy at the moment,' and the door was closed and locked.

George hammered on it again. 'No, you don't understand, I need to see the...Mr Bishop.'

He heard a muffled voice which he thought said, 'Go away, I'm just getting him into bed.'

Chapter 15

Alan could also hear a muffled voice, but his was coming from the bathroom and it was singing a rude rugby song punctuated with glugs from a bottle. He didn't think his single malt was going to last long at this rate.

He paced up and down outside the door tripping over Ping who was not best pleased and bit him on the ankle. Alan didn't even notice. He was too busy trying to decide what to do first. Should he go to the Vicarage to make sure George had got rid of everyone? Or should he drive the Bishop back to the palace and hope he'd forgotten all about his visit? Or should he ring Caroline?

The decision was finally made for him. When he rang, Caroline hadn't arrived at her hotel. He couldn't drive the Bishop back to the palace because his mother had taken the car; which left running through the village as fast as he could to check that George was doing what he'd promised.

Caroline arrived at the hotel in Oxford a few minutes after Alan's phone call. As she was unpacking, she saw through the window of her room the spire of Christ Church Cathedral towering over the college and had the same uneasy feeling she'd forgotten something.

She checked her suitcase – yes, she'd remembered her toothbrush and her nightdress and she must have got the right date otherwise she couldn't have booked in. So, what the heck was it?

George gave one last kick on Maddie's door and went downstairs. The weekend was turning into a disaster. As he reached the hall the phone rang. 'Kingsford Vicarage…Yes dear, I know what the time is…I'll be home in a minute and then I'll go straight to Nailsea to pay the caterers.' Before he could say any more his wife had ended the call.

Then he remembered he needed to find out why 'Meals-on-the-Move' hadn't arrived. When he'd made the booking, they had promised to be at the Vicarage by 10.30 at the latest, ready to offer coffee and home-made shortbread to the guests, before getting the lunch ready. But all he got was the answerphone. As it was a two-man band he hoped that meant they were on their way

He slammed the receiver down and looked around for someone to shout at. His prayers were answered - Alan came in the front door. 'Where the hell have you been?'

Alan was equally furious. 'Where the hell have I been! Where the hell have you been? The Bishop's drunk a bottle of my best malt and we have to get him back to the palace before mother comes home and wants to use the bathroom.'

'That's not the Bishop. The real Bishop Herbert arrived after you'd gone. He's now upstairs in that Maddie's bed.'

119

Alan didn't think things could get worse - but they had. He stared at George in horror. 'But how did he get in there?'

'It doesn't matter how he got in there, it's getting him out that's going to be the problem.'

'She's not in there with him, is she?'

'Possibly – I don't know.'

'We've got to get him out of there.'

'I know that, Alan. Only she's locked the door.'

Before Alan could ask any more questions, Dickie crossed the hall carrying a tray of coffee. 'So, how's your farmer friend, George? I take it that's where you went – or did you actually scrub Marigold's back?'

'Fine, yes, he's fine.'

'That's good. I said Maddie was a regular Florence Nightingale.' He paused outside the drawing room door. 'While I take this coffee into the ladies perhaps you could chivvy up the caterers.'

'Yes, I just have, and they're on their way.'

As soon as Dickie disappeared Alan demanded to know who the farmer friend was.

'I couldn't let on he was Bishop Herbert could I, so I said he was Herbert Bishop, a local farmer who likes dressing up.'

Alan shook his head in bewilderment. 'So, who's the bloke in my bathroom?'

'I think he's one of the actors, Ronald somebody or other.'

'What!' Alan couldn't believe he'd given his best whiskey to some drunken oaf involved in the murder mystery play.

'Talking of actors, three of Dickie's haven't turned up so I said we'd help out.'

Now Alan had heard it all. 'You are joking, aren't you?'

'All you have to do is pretend to be a vicar for the weekend.'

'Are you mad, I'm not doing that.'

Before George could plead with him Dickie came out of the drawing room. 'I've just had a thought, if Alan doesn't want to be the vicar, perhaps we could ask your farmer friend, as he likes dressing up. I'll go and have a word with him.' And having dropped that bombshell he headed towards the stairs.

Their earlier roles were now reversed and it was George who was hanging onto Dickie. 'No, no, Alan's keen to do it aren't you Alan? You love acting, don't you? You were in the amateur dramatic society, weren't you?'

Alan struggled to find the words. 'I...I...'

'See, he's overcome with excitement. He's really looking forward to it.'

'And I hope you're looking forward to doing the cooking, George, because if the caterers don't hurry up, you'll be getting lunch. After all you're the butler.'

'You're the butler.' For the first time that day Alan felt like laughing - and he did.

'I wouldn't laugh if I were you. The vicar's a woman, you'll be in drag.' And George dashed up the stairs.

'What!' And Alan dashed up after him.

Memories of Eastbourne crept into Dickie's mind as he headed towards the kitchen.

At the other end of the village Ronald, despite the amount of alcohol he'd consumed, was getting concerned. He'd been promised a dry pair of trousers, which hadn't arrived, but even more worrying he couldn't get out of the bathroom.

After singing a few verses of 'Three old ladies stuck in the lavatory' he started banging on the door. But all he could hear was a ferocious dog barking. He looked at the window, but it was hardly big enough to get his arm through.

He peered through the keyhole. Something was blocking it. Somewhere in the back of his whiskey-befuddled mind he remembered a part he'd played in a short-lived television series. His character had been trapped in a room, but had escaped by pushing the key out and catching it on a piece of paper. He tore a strip off the toilet roll and set to work.

On the other side of the door Ping watched with interest as a piece of toilet paper slid under it. He knew he wasn't allowed to pull paper off the toilet roll, but when a piece is pushed towards him, then, surely, he was allowed to play with that. He pounced on it, threw it in the air, tore it into shreds and ate it. Another piece appeared – oh joy, this was fun.

Alan caught up with George outside Maddie's bedroom. 'I told you to cancel this weekend and now you're expecting me to take part.'

'Only until we get the Bishop out of that room then I will tell everyone to go.' With his fingers still crossed, George rattled the door handle. 'Still locked.'

'What are they going in there?'

'I don't know.' George pulled Alan into the adjoining bedroom. 'We need something to hold against the wall.' He looked round and saw a crystal vase on the chest of drawers and clamped it to his ear. 'Nothing, I can't hear a thing. Is that good or bad?'

Alan slumped down on the bed, head between his knees. 'I still don't understand how he got in there in the first place.'

George explained what had happened earlier and ended by saying 'None of this would have happened if you'd kept a better look out for him when you were outside.'

Alan had had enough. 'I'm going to kill you for this.' As he bent forward to stand up, he saw under the bed the light glinting on a piece of rose-decorated porcelain and pulled it out.

Ronald had pushed nearly a whole roll of toilet paper under the door before the wretched dog finally stopped tearing each sheet to shreds, allowing him to retrieve the key. When he got the door open, he was warmly greeted by the Pekinese who then vomited up all the toilet paper it had eaten on his foot. Pushing the dog away he looked round for his trousers – wet or not he didn't want to leave without them.

But finding his trouser was the easy bit, he still had to negotiate the bridge over the stream again and then find his way back to the Vicarage. He guessed he was heading in the right direction when he saw the same group of villagers outside the Post Office who variously called out to him, 'Way to go Bish' and 'You'm a proper gent me dear', depending on their age.

The village wit said that he looked like a crane on crack, then hastily added not that he had ever taken crack or even knew what it was. Which saved him from a clip round the ear from his grandmother.

Ronald waved his arms again in a blessing and asked, 'Whither the Vicarage, my children?'

At first, they looked at him blankly as if he was speaking a foreign language, then one of them said, 'Do you mean where's it to?'

'If that is the local vernacular, yes.'

'Straight down that way.'

'Bless you, bless you,' and Ronald tottered off, his mitre at a rakish angle and his hairy, bare legs showing under his cope.

As he entered the front door of the Vicarage his welcome from Dickie was somewhat less warm. 'Where the devil have you been Ronald?'

'I was kidnapped dear boy.'

'Kidnapped, don't be ridiculous, who'd want to kidnap you?'

'I don't know. I expect it was for a ransom.'

'Ransom?'

Ronald tried to look imperious. 'Yes, after all, this weekend could not go on without me. I expect I'm worth thousands of pounds.' He swayed again. 'Tell you what, since I've saved you a fortune by escaping, could you see your way clear to giving me an advance?'

'Rubbish, you've been to the pub, you're drunk.'

'Absolutely not, cross my heart and hope to die.' Ronald was outraged, for once it was true, he hadn't crept out to go to the local hostelry.

'Look at you, you're wavering around all over the place.'

'That must be the drugs.'

'Drugs! You've been taking drugs?'

'No...yes. First of all, they tried to blindfold me with my mitre. Then they must have drugged me, because when I came round, I was locked in the bathroom of a strange house.'

'So how did you get away...from this strange house?'

'Luckily I had my wits about me.'

'Well, that'll be a first.'

Ronald looked offended. 'I shall ignore that remark. I remembered a scene I did in that television series - what was it called?'

'The Magic Roundabout?'

'No before that. Anyway, I did that old trick of pushing a piece of paper under the door and getting the key. Then I had to get past this vicious guard dog, huge it was, a monster...,'

'I don't believe a word of it. You'd better go and sober up.' Dickie stopped and stared at Ronald's legs. 'Where are your trousers? You've been shacked up with some woman, haven't you?'

'No, no I told you I was kidnapped.'

'I warned you about sleeping with the guests, so I'm docking part of your wages.'

Ronald was even more outraged, again he was innocent. He fumbled under the cope and pulled out the trousers he tied round his waist. 'See I still have my trousers.' He waved them in Dickie's face.

Dickie took a step back, they smelled awful. 'They're soaking wet, you'd better ask Marigold to wash them along with Charles.'

Ronald couldn't see that happening, but he could think of a way to distract Dickie from docking his money. Dickie loved gossip so he leaned towards him. 'There's something you should know Dickie - Charles didn't have laryngitis at all. That was just a cover story!'

'What do you mean?'

'Apparently,' Ronald leaned in closer, 'he's had the snip.'

'What are you talking about?'

'He's had a vasectomy.'

'No! Who told you?'

'The kidnappers.'

'The kidnappers? You're making this up.'

'It's true, cross my heart and hope to die. They said he'd had the operation so he couldn't have any more children after a misunderstanding with a Miss Jones.'

126

Ronald giggled, 'I thought his voice was higher. You can always tell.' Before he could say anymore Marigold came down the stairs.

'Dickie, I have to speak to you.'

'I thought you were getting changed.'

'My new lover is being chased along the landing by a complete stranger brandishing a chamber pot and shouting he's going to kill him. Would you kindly tell me what is going on?'

'That's not your new lover. That's George and Alan, they are taking over the roles of the Butler and the Vicar.'

'But what about Angus? And the others?'

'It appears they have found more lucrative employment. Bastards.'

'So, are these people actors?'

'No, of course they aren't.'

Marigold's voice dropped an octave. 'You're expecting me to work with... amateurs?' She swung round and glared at Ronald. 'Surely you won't agree to this?'

'Does that mean I'm back playing the Honourable Giles, Dickie?'

'No, Charles is. You are still a bishop, Ronald, so try to act like one.'

Marigold grabbed Ronald by the shoulders and shook him. 'Are you listening to me? We are professionals. We have standards to maintain.'

'Stop shouting Marigold I've got a headache.'

Seeing she was getting no support from Ronald she turned back to Dickie. 'So, if Lavinia isn't coming who is going to be my maid?'

'I am.'

'You!'

Ronald started sniggering again. 'Why don't you ask Charles to be to be the maid, after all he's the one with the girly voice.'

'Charles? What's happened to his voice?' Marigold glared at Dickie. 'Will you tell me what's going on or I swear I shall walk out.'

'According to Ronald, he's had a vasectomy.'

Marigold, who had always fancied Charles, was impressed. 'How considerate.'

Ronald suddenly felt very sick. He didn't know if it was the alcohol or the thought of having a vasectomy. 'I don't feel awfully well. I'm going to get my head down,' and he crawled up the stairs.

Marigold screamed after him, 'Don't you dare go in the bathroom, I have some washing soaking in there.'

And Dickie shouted, 'You've got five minutes to sober up and then we start acting.'

When Ronald had disappeared Marigold turned to Dickie, 'And there's another thing Dickie. While I was unpacking, I realised the plot won't work if the vicar is a woman.'

'Rubbish, of course it will.'

'No, it won't. The vicar kills Giles because he is in love with me and jealous of Giles being my lover. It won't work if the vicar is a woman.'

'It does work old love - it just means that you're a pair of…'

Before he could complete the sentence, Marigold said, 'Don't even think about it.' Then, taking a deep breath she headed for the stairs, 'And now I shall go and prepare myself for my performance.'

Dickie snorted, but didn't say anything as he followed her up the stairs. It was time for him to change into the maid's outfit and tell Charles he was now Sir Giles. At least someone would be happy.

Chapter 16

As Freda had predicted the ginger biscuits were stale and the coffee was virtually undrinkable, but the caffein had galvanised her. She paced up and down wondering what to do. She'd threatened to write to the Archbishop. So why not do it. He should be made aware of what was going on at this so-called retreat?

'I'm going to do it Angela, I'm going write to the Archbishop.'

'What are you going to say Freda?' Angela was awestruck she couldn't imagine ever writing to the Primate.

'I shall describe that disgraceful incident we witnessed earlier of course.' Her pacing got more agitated.

'But it was a farmer who got knocked out, not a real bishop.'

'Yes, Angela, I know that, but it was the Vicar who hit him – and a female vicar to boot. I don't think the Archbishop will condone that sort of behaviour amongst the clergy, even on a retreat.'

Angela could see an immediate problem, 'We don't have any writing paper…or… envelopes or… stamps.'

'Then we shall go and buy some.'

'But you don't have his address.'

Freda looked at her in exasperation, 'Of course I know his address.' What she didn't say was that she wrote to him quite frequently on matters all and sundry. 'He lives in Canterbury.'

Angela looked at her watch. She knew there was no stopping Freda once she got the bit between her teeth. 'But we don't know anywhere round here that sells stationery, wouldn't it be better to wait until we get home.' What she really wanted to say was I don't want to miss lunch even if it is some strange vegetarian concoction. Freda had told her not to expect normal food this weekend - something to do with flagellating the body to purify the soul, though where her sister got this information from Angela had no idea.

Freda abruptly stopped pacing. 'This is a village Angela and villages have Post Offices and Post Offices sell all those things. Come along.'

Angela looked out of the window and had one last try, 'I think it's started to rain again. Shall we wait until after lunch.'

'A little bit of rain won't hurt us, we've got coats. And as for lunch, well you can forget that.' And with one brisk movement she swept out of the drawing room, grabbed their coats from the newel post and pushed Angela out of the front door.

Once again Freda found herself outside the Vicarage, with no clear idea where she was going and rain easing its way down her neck. She had spoken boldly about every village having a Post Office from the comfort of the drawing room, but now she was outside - looking at muddy grass verges and the calling cards from a herd of cows which had passed by recently - she wasn't so sure. But Freda never backed away from a challenge so squaring her shoulders she set off down the road as if she had an intimate knowledge of Kingsford's topography. Angela gave one last, longing glance back at the Vicarage where it was at least warm and dry and set off after her.

Freda, of course was right to surmise that Kingsford had a Post Office, and the Post Mistress was doing a roaring trade with her coffee and cakes. The villagers were still talking about Ronald. To have such a spectacle twice in one day was unheard of treasure. Nothing was left unremarked on from the church warden lurching through the village with a bishop hanging round his neck, to sometime later, the bishop running back without his trousers in apparent pursuit of the church warden, who had a good head start.

There were dark mutterings such as 'what is the world coming to' and 'things have come to a pretty pass.' Various theories were put forward. One group blamed the behaviour on the England football team's shock defeat by Norway in last year's World Cup qualifiers. Another group thought the recent opening of the Channel Tunnel was to blame and there was total agreement that joining England with France was not a good idea. A local historian even shouted, 'Did the Battle of Agincourt stand for nothing?' Finally, a lone voice said it was because Edvard Munch's painting 'The Scream' had been stolen earlier in the year. But no one took any notice of him because no one else had heard of Edvard Munch.

132

There was however a consensus of opinion that while bishops might act in strange ways, both church wardens could be relied on to behave with a sense of decorum.

In the Vicarage, George and Alan were still fighting for control of the chamber pot when they heard Marigold storming back up the stairs closely followed by Dickie. Ducking back into the room next door to Maddie's they saw her go into the bathroom, lock the door and start on a series of voice exercises. After banging on the bathroom door and telling her to be quick Dickie went on past and up to the attic.

They were just about to creep out when Maddie came out of her bedroom carrying a vanity case and tried the bathroom door. A voice told her to 'piss off' and then went back to making strange gargling sounds. Hoping there was a cloakroom somewhere she went down stairs.

George watched until she had disappeared then closely followed by Alan, still brandishing the chamber pot they, crept into her room.

Bishop Herbert was curled up under the covers snoring gently. George grabbed his shoulder and shook it. He opened one eye and looked at them nervously, particularly at Alan, who hurriedly put the pot under Maddie's bed. 'Who are you?'

George tried to help him up. 'We're the Church Wardens.'

Herbert felt about in the bedclothes. 'Where are my glasses?'

'I think they got broken My Lord.'

'What? When?'

'You dropped them when you arrived. Don't you remember?'

'No, I don't.'

George looked at Alan and gave a brief smile. It looked as if Herbert had lost his memory. 'You go and check the coast is clear and I'll bring him down,' he whispered.

A querulous voice rose from the duvet, 'What are you whispering about?'

'Nothing, My Lord. Now let me help you up.'

Alan rushed down the stairs and checked the hall; then he rushed back up again. 'It's okay, there's no one around.'

Between them they manoeuvred Herbert out of Maddie's room. But Herbert wasn't going quietly. 'Where are you taking me?'

George whispered, 'We're taking you home, My Lord.'

'Speak up I can't hear you.'

George shouted in his ear. 'We're taking you home.'

'There's no need to shout, I'm not deaf I've just broken my glasses.'

To get down the stairs they had to go in single file with Herbert sandwiched between them. 'Watch how you go, sir.' Alan didn't want the myopic Bishop missing his footing and sending them both crashing to the hall.

But Herbert was still resisting and refused to move. 'I haven't had a talk with my new vicar yet, we only had the briefest of meetings just now.'

George gave him a nudge from behind and got him down another step. 'Can you remember much about that?'

'No, I can't remember a thing after saying "ah the good lady herself".'

'Oh, good.'

'Pardon?'

'Good...yes, the good lady herself, the Reverend Caroline Timberlake.' George gave another nudge and they got down another step, but at this rate it was going to take all the morning to get him to the front door.

'But now I am now fully recovered and ready to commence my duties. However, I would appreciate it if nothing more was said about this morning's unfortunate occurrence, although it was quite a blow to me.'

'It certainly was,' George muttered.

'I beg your pardon.'

'It certainly was ... is. It is certainly is generous of you, My Lord, to want to forget about it.' He gave another nudge, they got down another step and then another.

Halfway down the flight Herbert stopped again. 'I don't mind telling you it was a bit of a shock coming round in a strange women's bed. I had hoped there would be no more of these episodes.'

Alan was shocked, how many strange women's beds had he been in?

'My doctors warned me I mustn't get too excited or I could temporarily pass out - high blood pressure or something. Load of nonsense of course, what do they know about it?'

George tried to get him moving again and said sympathetically, 'Well, sometimes they get it right, My Lord.'

And Alan added, not quite so sympathetically, 'So perhaps it would be best if you went straight home.'

'Rubbish. When I say I'll do something, I do it - and I am here to meet my new vicar and nothing is going to stop me.'

'But you've already had a very long chat with her My Lord.'

Herbert turned and glared at George. 'No, I haven't.'

'I expect you've temporarily forgotten it, sir. I'm sure it will all come back to you when you get back to the palace.'

Herbert turned and glared at Alan. 'I know whether I've had a chat or not and I definitely haven't had a long chat with the Rev Timberlake. For a start I want to say I will give her all the support she needs. And I also want to know how she is going to raise the money for the church roof fund. She can't expect the diocese to cough up. Now, where is she? What's the hold-up?'

'There's no hold-up sir…it just that…,'

Worried about what Alan might say under stress – the phone call with Miss Jones fresh in his mind – George quickly added, 'I'm afraid she's been taken ill.'

'Rubbish there was nothing wrong with her when we met earlier. Our meeting might have been brief, but I remember she looked full of health.'

By this time, they had reached the bottom of the stairs and Alan was about to open the front door when Maddie appeared from the cloakroom.

Working as a team George and Alan pushed Herbert back hard against a wall and stood in front of him trying to look nonchalant.

'Hello you two.' She stood, appraising them, 'you have a guilty look about you. What have you been up to?'

'Nothing. Nothing guilty at all.' Alan was struggling to hold Herbert upright, but he kept sagging.

George glanced over his shoulder and saw the bishop was unconscious again. 'What gives you that idea?'

'Let's just say a woman's intuition. But I'd better get back to my Bishop, he might have come round by now.'

They waited until she had disappeared and then stepped away from Herbert who slid to the floor.

George gently kicked his leg, there was no response. 'Now what's the matter with him?'

Alan picked up the fallen picture of the 'Stag at Bay' and rehung it. 'This must have hit him on the head.' The animal had finally got its revenge on the human race.

'The man's a walking disaster.'

'We can't take him back to the palace unconscious.'

'Yes, we can, the fresh air will bring him round. Look outside see if the coast is clear.'

Alan peered out of the front door and heard voices in the lane. 'I think there's someone coming.'

'Damn! Quick, get him into the library, while I'll get rid of them.'

137

'Why don't I get rid of them while you take him to the library?'

'After the problem you caused talking to Miss Jones. I don't think that's a good idea, do you?'

Alan was miffed, 'So then what do I do with him?'

'Give me five minutes and when the coast is clear I'll get his car and you can drive him home.'

Still Alan hesitated. 'What shall I say to him if he comes round?'

'Tell him he's had another black out. He seems to expect them, doesn't he?'

'But only if he gets annoyed.'

'Well annoy him then. That shouldn't be difficult. Heaven knows you're annoying me at the moment.'

Alan glared at him. 'And if that doesn't work?'

'Threaten him with this,' and with a flourish George pulled the gun out of his pocket.

Alan took several steps back, 'I can't do that.'

'Can you think of a better idea? No, so quick, get him into the library I can hear them coming up the path.'

Alan laid the gun on Herbert's chest and dragged him into the library. Herbert's feet had scarcely vanished round the corner when Freda and Angela came in the front door.

138

Chapter 17

In the attic Dickie was giving his actors a good talking to, but Ronald had fallen asleep and Marigold, having been dragged out of the bathroom, was looking mutinous. Only Charles was pleased with the change of plan and the fancy cravat Dickie had given him. His only concern was what trousers he could wear. Even if he got his luggage, he didn't have a spare pair and Marigold was not the domestic goddess she claimed to be – his trousers were still as muddy as ever, but now even wetter. And his shoes were in pretty much the same state as well.

As Dickie hopped about on one foot trying to change into tights and a little black dress with frilly apron, Marigold launched another tirade on having to work with amateurs. 'If this got out, I would be a laughing stock.'

Ronald managed to wake up long enough to say she already was. And when Dickie asked if he could borrow a pair of her shoes, she was so busy trying to suffocate Ronald with a pillow that he was able to look in her suitcase and find a pair of sandals without her noticing. Luckily, she had large feet so he was able to force them on and head downstairs.

As soon as he'd gone Charles grabbed Dickie's trousers and shoes and finished getting dressed.

Freda and Angela's visit to the Post Office had not been totally successful. For a start, they hadn't expected to run the gauntlet of local residents, but Freda soon silenced them with one of her glares. Inside, the Post Mistress apologised, 'Tis not often we has so many strangers in the village so they'm a bit over-excited like.'

While Freda was looking for writing paper and envelopes, Angela managed to buy a large piece of ginger cake to stave off any hunger pangs. The stationery wasn't what Freda would have chosen but it was all the Post Office had.

As they set off back to the Vicarage, they were again the objects of speculation and the Post Mistress had to come out and tell the villagers what the two old dears had bought - which set off another round of discussion.

Once in the front door, Freda whipped off her coat, and grabbing Angela's, handed them to a surprised George. 'Ah George, perhaps you would care to take our coats and hang them up.'

George threw them half onto the newel post. 'There you are…Madam.'

'We could have done that. I meant hang them up properly.'

'Well, it's where you hung them just now.' But before he could escape through the front door an apparition in a French maid's outfit grabbed him by the wrist and then gave a quick curtsey to the open-mouthed sisters.

'Quick,' Dickie hissed at George, 'introduce me as Lydia, Lady Alicia's maid.'

George, who was as equally transfixed as the sisters, managed to mutter. 'This is Lydia, Lady Alicia's maid.'

Angela curtseyed back. 'Pleased to meet you I'm sure.' Freda sniffed with derision.

Dickie strangled his larynx, coughed up the human equivalent of a fur ball and in a stumbling falsetto said, 'Thank you, Madam.' Then he surreptitiously passed a script across to George and whispered, 'Right, we'll act out a little scene for them as practice - start reading from page eight.'

Angela and Freda after the first shock of meeting Lady Alicia's maid busied themselves with tidying up their coats and taking writing paper and envelopes out of a carrier bag.

Checking they could hear him Dickie, once again in his falsetto with an excruciating fake cockney accent, said, 'Dearest George, the Honourable Giles Forsythe is blackmailing me. I know I should never have stolen Lady Alicia's diamond necklace, but he said my mother was ill with consumption. How was I to know it was consumption of too much gin? Ow, ow, ow, whatever shall I do?'

He took another glance at Angela and Freda to check their reaction and was pleased to see that although they were pretending to be preoccupied with their writing paper, they were hanging on his every word.

George was still trying to edge out of the front door. 'I'm sorry, but you'll have to sort it out yourself, I've got to pop off for a minute.'

'That's not in the script; do it properly.' Dickie gave the front door a push, locked it and put the key down the front of his blouse.

George sighed and in a monotone voice read, 'The foul swine. I would gladly spend all my savings replacing the necklace if that would stop the Honourable Giles or should I say dishonourable Giles from pursuing you and forcing his foul intentions on you.'

'No please, do not do that for I fear that even if the necklace is replaced, I will never escape from his evil clutches. Sometimes I feel there is only one way out for me.' Dickie wasn't sure how long he could keep the falsetto going – the Bee Gees had made it seem so easy in 'Saturday Night Fever'

'I would do anything Lydia to free you from his evil clutches.'

Dickie flung himself into George's arms. 'Oh George, my hero. If only we could be together forever and ever.'

George struggled to follow the script with Dickie hanging round his neck. 'Then we must leave and go where he cannot find us.'

'No, no, I could never leave Lady Alicia, I owe it to her to stay and try to open her eyes to what sort of man her lover is, perhaps then she will forgive me my crime. Come let us go into the kitchen.'

'That's not in the script...'

'It is now,' Dickie hissed, 'because if the caterers haven't arrived, we've got to get the lunch started,' and he pulled a reluctant George out of the hall.

A shocked Freda waited until they had disappeared before asking Angela if she'd heard what they were saying. As Angela was too shocked to speak Freda added, 'If we've got to put up with this sort of thing, we should ask for an even bigger refund. And I shall add it to my letter to the Archbishop.'

Before she could say anymore Maddie came down the stairs. She was still thoroughly enjoying herself even though her bishop had gone awol.

Seeing the sisters, she said, 'Hello you two. Isn't this fun?'

Freda and Angela stared at her in amazement. Fun was the last thing they could think of. Freda decided it was her duty to tell her what was going on. 'We could not help overhearing Lady Alicia's maid and butler having a private conversation just now.'

'Not that we normally listen to what other people are saying you understand.' Angela didn't want her to think they were always so nosey.

'Quite Angela. And putting two and two together I would say that Lady Alicia's maid is being blackmailed by the Honourable Giles Forsythe; whoever he is.'

Far from being shocked they were surprised to find Maddie full of enthusiasm. 'How exciting, I just adore titled men.'

Thinking perhaps Maddie hadn't fully grasped the seriousness of the situation, Freda added, 'Don't you think there are some very strange people here? And what about that woman saying she was locked in the attic?'

The sisters had discussed Marigold's claim of imprisonment and wondered if it was part of being on a retreat, after all they'd never been on one before so perhaps it was.

'I think one just has to go with the flow and see what happens.'

'We don't intend going with the flow, we are going into the library to write everything down.'

It was at that moment Alan had crept out of the library to see where George had got to. When he heard where Freda and Angela were planning to write their letter he ducked back again pretty quickly.

Maddie thought taking notes was a brilliant idea. 'I shall do the same and then we can compare. Now I must go and look for George and Alan, I think they might be in the drawing room.' She paused in the doorway and draped herself dramatically against the door frame. 'You never know they could even be the murderers.' And she shut the door.

'Murderers! Oh Freda, we might be horribly murdered in our beds.'

'We'd be entitled to a full refund then, Angela. But first I need my fountain pen it's in my suitcase.' And she led the way upstairs at a run.

Chapter 18

In the library, Alan was trying to find somewhere to hide the unconscious Herbert, without success. He finally sat him in an armchair and sat on top of him just in case Freda and Angela came in. When no one came, he had another quick look in the hall. It was empty.

Hoping that George had brought Herbert's car round he once again balanced the gun on Herbert's stomach and dragged him out of the library, but before he could get as far as the front door, he saw the drawing room door opening. With a presence of mind, he didn't normally possess, he grabbed the gun and put it down his trousers, grabbed Freda and Angela's coats from the newel post and threw them over the bishop and then adopted a nonchalant pose.

'Ah, there you are Alan.' Maddie tapped him playfully on the arm. 'Have you seen the Bishop?'

'Bishop?'

'Yes, he's disappeared.'

'Are you sure?'

'Yes, I've searched everywhere.' Maddie moved in closer, 'Why don't you give me a little clue about what's going on?'

'I can't.'

'Can't, or won't.'

'I'm as much in the dark as you are.'

'Of course, I keep forgetting, you didn't see what happened earlier did you?'

Alan was about to explain that George had told him when Maddie said, 'Come into the drawing room and I'll reveal all.'

'What! No, certainly not.'

'I thought you'd like a debrief.' When Maddie saw he'd gone as red as a beetroot, she quickly added, 'Sorry only my little joke.'

Alan relaxed and tried a little joke of his own, 'I'll keep my briefs on then if it's all right with you.'

Maddie smiled, 'Now, I wonder where the Bishop fits into all this.'

'Bishop? What bishop? I haven't seen a bishop.'

Herbert chose that moment to groan, very loudly.

Maddie looked round with suspicion. 'What was that?'

Alan didn't think he could cope with much more. Where the hell was George with the car?

There was another groan from under the coats. Alan stamped his legs vigorously. 'It was me I've got cramp.'

'Oh, I know just the thing for cramp.'

'I rather thought you might.' He shook each leg again. 'It's all right; it's better now.'

But Maddie was not to be denied a second chance of practicing first aid. 'Stand still you silly man. Now which leg was it?' And she knelt down in front of him.

Alan tried to back towards the stairs and bumped into Freda and Angela on their way back down. 'She's just giving me a massage! For cramp!'

146

Freda gave a disbelieving sniff as she and Angela headed towards the library. 'Is that what you call it?'

Alan was torn, he couldn't leave Herbert on the other hand he didn't want them writing to the Archbishop. 'No stop.' He tried to walk after them forgetting Maddie was kneeling in front of him. A professional rugby tackle couldn't have brought him down better.

Maddie stood up, pulling a groggy Alan up with her. 'Oh, let them get on with it. We all have our different ways of working things out.'

'But they're writing to the Archbishop.'

'Well let them, but I don't think he'll be able to give them any clues. How's your cramp?'

'Fine, absolutely fine.'

Another muffled groan from Herbert again triggered Maddie's nursing zeal. 'I knew you'd hurt your arm. Now, what we need is a sling. Hang on a minute I'll just tear my dress up and make one.' And she started pulling her dress over her head. As fast as she was pulling it up Alan was trying to pull it down again.

Angela and Freda stood watching them from the library door. Angela was holding out a sheet of writing paper embellished with kittens in baskets playing with balls of wool. It wasn't what Freda had in mind for writing to the Archbishop and she hoped he would forgive her.

'We thought you'd like some of our paper.'

'I don't think she's planning to write anything at the moment, Angela.'

This was true as Maddie and Alan were still engaged in an energetic tussle with her dress.

A shocked Angela and Freda shut themselves in the library. Freda slammed the piece of writing paper down on the desk and grasping her fountain pen firmly, began her letter 'Dear Very Reverend…,' but the thought of what was happening in the hall kept floating before her eyes.

Had the sisters stayed they would have seen Maddie changing tactics. She stopped trying to get her dress off and was trying to undress Alan instead so that she could use his jacket sleeve as a sling. This required pulling him close, very close. 'Oh, if I didn't know you better, I'd say you had a gun in your pocket.'

'What! No.' Alan squirmed - he couldn't admit to having a gun. Squeezing his eyes so tightly it hurt the back of his head he said, 'No…I'm just pleased to see you.'

Maddie stepped back surprised. 'Oh, Alan.'

In that moment, Alan managed to spin round, wrench off his jacket and create his own sling. 'Thank you, this feels much better, no pain at all.' He hoped Herbert wouldn't spoil the effect by groaning again. 'Don't you think you should be looking for your bishop, I'm sure he could do with some attention.'

Maddie pouted. 'I would if I could find him.'

'Perhaps he's gone back to your bed. Why don't you go and see?'

'I think you know more than you're letting on, Alan. Still, I can take a hint. Bye for now.' And to Alan's relief

148

she went upstairs. As soon as she'd disappeared, he dragged Herbert into the drawing room.

And not a second too soon because Freda had managed to dash off a strongly worded missive in record time and was determined to get it in the post. She looked round the hall suspiciously. 'Good, they've gone.'

'I wonder what they're doing now?'

'I don't think we want to know that, Angela.'

Angela would have loved to know, but from ingrained habit replied, 'No, of course not, Freda.'

Freda checked her watch. 'Right, we'll just have time to post this before lunch.' She headed for the newel post to collect her coat, but stopped so suddenly Angela bumped into her. 'Our coats have gone.'

'Perhaps we left them upstairs.'

'No, we gave them to the butler person and he threw them onto this post.' Freda glared at the newel post and then round the hall.

'I expect he's hung them up somewhere then.'

'Nonsense Angela, they have been stolen.'

Now Angela was looking round the hall. 'Who'd want to steal them?'

'I don't know, but I did have copy of the Bradford bus timetable in my pocket.'

'I've changed my mind Freda I don't think we ought to stay here. It was bad enough with murderers and blackmailers but now there are thieves as well.'

Freda straightened her shoulders. 'No Angela, we owe it to the Archbishop to get to the bottom of this.' And holding the letter out in front of her like a crusader's sword, she declaimed, 'We don't need coats,' and sallied forth. Luckily the sun had come out again.

Chapter 19

As soon as Alan heard the front door slam shut, he peered out of the drawing room and seeing the hall was once again empty put the sisters' coats back on the newel post. After waving the gun round looking for somewhere to hide it, he finally dropped into Freda's coat pocket. Then he shot back into the drawing room and locked the door.

After dragging Herbert round the room several times, he tucked him behind one of the settees and covered him with cushions. Then he flung himself into an armchair and cursed George for taking so long to get the car.

In the kitchen George was frantically looking through Caroline's fridge in the hope of finding something for lunch. Dickie had once again asked where the caterers were and George once again said he'd rung them and they were on their way.

His search was proving fruitless - all he had come up with so far were some sad looking salad ingredients, a chunk of cheddar cheese and half a dozen eggs. The freezer was a bit more promising with two different kinds of ice cream, a bag of oven chips and a sliced loaf.

Dickie was having better luck in the larder if all the guests liked baked beans, tinned pineapple and evaporated milk.

'So, what are you going to make for us then George?'

'Me! I can't cook, that's my wife's department.'

'You'd better ring her then and ask her to come over.'

'Ah...no, she's out for the day.' The last thing George wanted was his wife coming down to the vicarage.

Dickie looked at what they'd found. Being a bachelor, he was used to knocking up meals out of nothing. 'We'll make cheese sandwiches, dip them in egg and fry them. Chop up that salad stuff and we'll use that as a garnish.' He glared at George. 'But if the caterers don't arrive with a substantial evening meal you won't be getting paid.'

Maddie sat on her bed feeling lonely. She wasn't normally given to introspection but occasionally, like now, she thought about her late husband who had adored her. Twenty years her senior, he'd had the good manners to die quietly at the age of sixty-nine, leaving her with a charming house in Surrey and sufficient money to indulge most if not all her whims.

She wished he was here with her now, but then of course she wouldn't be here if Dennis was still alive. A man more interested in the Financial Times and a Sunday round of golf than the theatre, a murder mystery weekend was the last thing he would want to go to.

She was beginning to have a few misgivings herself, but she had tried dating agencies and singles holidays in the hope of meeting someone so this was her last fling so as to speak.

Ronald, sticking to Dickie's edict, not to use the bathroom, was on his way to the cloakroom, wrapped up in his cope. His trousers were still in the corner of the

152

attic where Marigold had thrown them when he asked her to wash them, and Charles had grabbed Dickie's pair before he could.

As he passed Maddie's open door, he heard a little sob and looked in, 'Having a problem dear lady?'

Maddie immediately brightened up. 'Oh, you're back. Do you know where the other bishop is?'

'The other bishop?' Ronald managed to look both affronted and suitably high church, which wasn't easy with his bare legs showing under the cope. 'What do you mean?'

'There's another bishop staying here, didn't you know?'

'No, I did not.' Ronald was outraged. 'I was only missing for two minutes and tricky Dickie gets someone else to take over my role. Where is this impostor?'

'He was in my bed earlier.'

'Good heavens woman, you don't waste any time. The minute my back is turned, you switch your allegiance.'

'I was only trying to give him first aid, but he's disappeared, I hope he's alright.'

'He won't be alright when I find him. I shall hunt him down and unfrock him or whatever has to be done to impostors.'

Maddie thought she ought to keep Ronald with her until he'd calmed down a bit. 'And I will help you, so why don't you come and sit on the bed and we can plan our campaign.'

Ronald wasn't sure that was a good idea. He didn't want Dickie to catch him in flagrante, he might not believe that Ronald, once again was the innocent party.

'Ah, perhaps not dear lady,'

But Maddie was stronger than she looked and Ronald found himself being pulled inside.

Chapter 20

Now that they knew their way to the Post Office, Freda and Angela's trip to post their letter was much quicker. Several villagers waved to them as they went inside to buy a first-class stamp. And after they'd gone the Post Mistress again reported on their purchase.

No one could remember the last time a first-class stamp had been bought, and there were mutterings about 'some people having money to burn' and 'wasteful extravagance'.

The first thing Freda saw as they entered the front door were their raincoats back on the newel post. She immediately checked her pocket for the Bradford bus timetable. Her fingers closed around something cold and hard. Bemused, she pulled it out.

'Freda! What are you doing with a gun?'

'Stop shrieking Angela I'm not doing anything with it.' Freda made a point of never being surprised – not by small boys with cricket balls stuck in their mouths or bigger boys snorting cocaine or parents threatening blackmail if she expelled their hooligan offspring. 'What I want to know is what is it doing in my pocket?'

But Angela couldn't stop shrieking. 'I didn't know you had a gun. Why do you need a gun? Why did you bring it with you? Oh, my goodness, I'm going to faint.'

She would have carried on in this vein for some time if Freda hadn't clamped a hand over her mouth. 'Pull yourself together Angela, of course it's not mine.'

'Well, whose is it? Suppose it's been used to murder someone. And now it's got your finger prints on it. Oh, Freda, the police will think you're a murderer.' Angela's words were a bit garbled as they tried to wriggle their way between Freda's fingers.

Before Freda could answer Dickie came out of the kitchen looking smug. After finding a packet of gelatine, which was only four months past its sell by date, he had used it to make a quick soufflé out of the pineapple and evaporated milk – and if he said so himself it tasted pretty good. Now he needed to make sure that the rest of his cast were dressed for their parts and ready to start acting.

Freda quickly pushed the gun into her cardigan and folded her arms over it to hide the bulge. 'Try to act naturally,' she hissed to Angela, 'we don't want to make her suspicious.'

'Ah Miss Andrews, Mrs Mortimer.' Dickie suddenly remembered he was supposed to be the maid so pushed his voice up an octave and gave a quick bob. 'I have some good news for you; the Rev Thorn is now a man.'

'A man?'

'Yes Miss Andrews, it was all a mistake we thought he was a woman but when the Bishop unfrocked him, we found he wasn't.'

Angela's voice also shut up an octave. 'You mean he's changed sex?'

'In a manner of speaking, yes.'

'This is most irregular.' Freda was so incensed she nearly put her hands on her hips but remembered the gun just in time.

'Perhaps you should write to the Archbishop again Freda.'

'There's no need to do that Mrs Mortimer...,' Dickie heard a noise on the stairs and looked up to see Ronald in all his glory with his bare legs sticking out from under his cope. Hoping the sisters hadn't noticed them he quickly added, 'when we have our very own Bishop Ronald.'

Ronald had managed to persuade Maddie they would be more comfortable sharing his bottle of gin in the drawing room. Pausing halfway down to ensure he had everyone's attention he quickly slipped into his role.

'Ah dear ladies, bless you, bless you.'

Angela looked at Ronald closely. 'Is this one real or just pretending like the other one?'

Ronald was incensed and glared at Dickie. 'So, it's true what this dear lady has been telling me,' and he turned and patted Maddie's arm, 'you *have* taken on another person to act as Bishop in my absence.'

'Oh, no, Your Grace, he was just some harmless old farmer who likes to dress up now and again. You know what they are like in the country.'

'No, young lady, I can't say as I do.'

Freda glared at Ronald. 'Well, Bishop there's something we want to make quite clear don't we Angela? We don't hold with ordination of women.'

Ronald beamed at her. 'No more do I, dear lady, no more do I.'

Dickie forced his voice up again, 'So, Your Grace, I was just telling Miss Andrews and Mrs Mortimer that the vicar has now changed sex.'

Ronald sniggered, 'Has he? I was told it was just the snip. Well, well, well.'

Freda wasn't yet ready to be mollified. 'Yes, well, we're pleased to hear the situation has changed aren't we Angela?'

But Angela wasn't listening she was wondering how the vicar had managed to change sex so quickly. Surely it was more than just a snip. Didn't it involve some sort of reconstructive surgery?

Maddie was getting bored and really needed a gin so she pulled at Ronald's arm. 'Come along Bishop let's find somewhere comfortable to sit.'

'So, it's back to normal everyone,' Dickie then remembered he was supposed to be a lowly maid so quickly bobbed a curtsey all round and added, 'begging your pardon.' He tried to get past Ronald and head for the dining room to lay the table.

But Ronald was having far too much fun. It wasn't often he could embarrass Dickie and get his own back for all the slights and digs he'd endured over the years. He placed himself firmly in front of Dickie, ignoring Maddie's tug on his arm, and declaimed, 'Right young lady, to show there are no hard feelings, you may kiss my ring,' and he stuck out his hand.

'Pardon.'

'It is customary for the maid to kiss the bishop's ring.'

158

Dickie ignored the digit with the knuckle duster Ronald always wore on his right-hand pinkie and hissed, 'Watch it or you won't get paid.'

'Ah, the wages of sin is death, young lady,' he boomed and chucked Dickie under the chin, 'Romans, chapter six, verse twenty three.' Even Ronald was surprised he knew that.

'Your career will be dead if you carry on hamming like this.'

But Ronald was beyond reasoning with. All the roles he had played in his short career on the London stage were flooding through his mind, he walked round the hall and striking a dramatic pose, he thundered, 'Dead and never called me mother.'

A shocked Freda whispered to Angela, 'I don't think the vicar's the only one who's changed sex.'

Ronald swung round and pointed a finger straight at Freda's chest. 'Murder, most foul.'

The sisters clutched each other in horror. 'Oh, Freda, he knows, he knows.'

Ronald walked towards them. 'Is this a dagger I see before me?'

Angela knew you must never lie to a bishop so she whispered, 'No it's a gun.'

'Angela! How could you.' A mortified Freda clutched her arms even tighter across her chest and backed away from Ronald.

'Funny, I could have sworn it used to be a dagger.' Ronald pushed the mitre up and scratched his head. 'Still, it matters not,' and lifting his arm up dramatically he declaimed, 'You who are about to die, I salute you.'

The reaction he got to this speech was most gratifying. Freda and Angela screamed and tried to jump into each other's arms.

Not wanting to miss out on the fun Maddie decided to join in as well. She pulled Ronald away from the sisters and declaimed, 'Eat, drink and be merry for tomorrow we die.' Which caused even more terror for Freda and Angela.

Ronald held her hand, gazed into her eyes and sang, 'Drink, drink, drink to eyes that are…'

He didn't get any further because Dickie was hissing in his ear, 'Perhaps a little less drinking would be a good idea Your Grace.'

Maddie was now fed up with talking about drinking and pulled Ronald firmly towards the drawing room. 'So, now that's all sorted out shall we go in here and sit down, Bishop?' But try as she might the door wouldn't open.

On the other side Alan watched with horror as the handle was fiercely yanked up and down and prayed the lock would hold.

'Oh dear, it's stuck. Never mind we can go and sit in the dining room.' And she pulled the reluctant Ronald into the room next door.

'Don't forget the rest of your flock, Your Grace; they will all want to meet you.' Dickie shouted after them.

'Now what's the problem with this door?' he rattled the drawing room handle but it wouldn't budge. 'I expect it needs a bit of oil. I've got some in my car. Won't be a moment, ladies.' And after another quick bob, which were playing havoc with his knees, he rushed outside.

Angela was first to speak. 'I don't want to die Freda - I want to go home.'

'Pull yourself together, Angela. If we leave now, we will be the prime suspects.'

'But what are we going to do about the gun?'

Freda pulled it out of her cardigan and looked at it. 'We've got to get rid of it.'

'How?'

'We'll post it to the police with an anonymous note.'

'But we don't have any wrapping paper.'

'We'll use what Barbara wrapped your present up in.'

'But I haven't opened it yet. My birthday's not until tomorrow.' Angela was a stickler for protocol

'We could be in prison by tomorrow, Angela.'

Angela decided that going to prison was as bad as being murdered so she followed Freda up to their bedroom.

Chapter 21

As soon as George realised that Dickie wasn't coming straight back, he stopped chopping salad and peered out into the hall to check if the coast was clear.

At the very same moment Alan peered out of the drawing room. 'Where the hell have you been? And why are you wearing a pinny?

'The caterers haven't shown up, I had to help Dickie start getting lunch ready.'

'Lunch! It doesn't matter about lunch. Have you moved the Bishop's car round the back?'

'Not exactly, I've had another idea Alan.'

'I liked the first idea, so let's just get him out of the drawing room and into his car.'

'What's he doing in the drawing room anyway?'

Alan sighed all these questions were wasting time. 'I had to move him; those old biddies said they were going in the library.'

'They didn't see him, did they?'

'No, but they've written a letter to the Archbishop about what's going on here.'

'What! Why didn't you stop them?' George rolled his hands up in the pinnie, reminding Alan of his grandmother on his paternal side.

'You said look after the Bishop, while you sorted out his car.'

George unrolled his hands. 'Is he still unconscious?'

'Sort of half and half.'

'If he's still groggy, we might get away with it - as long as we keep our nerve.'

'My nerve went a long time ago, let's just move him.'

'Look, the only way we are going to get rid of the Bishop and get Caroline off the hook is if he actually meets her.'

'Brilliant, but she's not here.'

'No, but that actor Charles is and the Bishop has already met him once and thinks he's Caroline.'

Alan felt his legs go weak. 'It won't work.'

'Yes, it will. Look, he's as blind as a bat without his glasses.'

'Who Charles?'

'No, the Bishop. We'll just ask him to stay dressed as a woman and have a quick chat.'

'Who the Bishop?' Alan had a vision of Herbert in drag and it wasn't pretty.

'No, Charles. We'll tell him the sort of things the Bishop wants to hear and then he can go on his way rejoicing.'

'Who Charles?'

'No, the Bishop.'

'And if he won't.'

'Offer him some money.'

'Who, the Bishop?' Alan was sure there was some ecclesiastical law against bribing bishops.

'No, Charles. Concentrate for goodness' sake.'

Alan was struggling to keep up with George's line of thought, but about one thing he was clear, he was not paying out any money – not to the Bishop, not to any actor, not to anyone. And he made this very plain to George.

George glared at him. 'Well, I haven't got any money. If I had any money, I wouldn't be in this mess in the first place.'

'Let this be a lesson to you George.'

'Save the sermon till later.' George decided Alan was sounding a bit too smug - it was time to put the boot in. 'So, you're not prepared to pay out a few miserable pounds to help Caroline. Well, well, well; and I thought you'd do anything for her.' He turned away and smoothed down his apron. 'Poor woman, she's only been here a few weeks and she's already in trouble with the Bishop.' He took a quick glance over his shoulder, was Alan weakening? 'I wouldn't be surprised if he didn't suggest she resigned and moved to another diocese.'

Alan couldn't face the thought of never again seeing Caroline standing in the pulpit, her cheeks flushed and her golden hair curling over her shoulders. 'A few pounds you said.'

'Yes.'

'How few?'

'Better make it fifty.'

'What! That isn't a few, that's a fortune.'

'You want to help Caroline, don't you?'

Alan reluctantly counted out five ten-pound notes.

George hurriedly pocketed them and then pushed Alan towards the drawing room. 'Now go back in there and keep an eye on him and I'll go and look for Charles.'

164

As soon as he heard Alan lock the door he sprinted upstairs.

Thus, missing Dickie coming in the front door with an oil can. He'd been delayed by calls on his mobile phone. 'Smythe-Hickson here old man. Got caught up in some damn diversions and have no idea where we are, but we're sitting in a pub and we think it might be Hinkley Point as we can see the power station in the distance. To cut a long story short we're going to have an early lunch and try to find our way later.'

As that meant two people less for lunch at the Vicarage Dickie told them not to worry. But no sooner had that call ended then he had another one, the dentist from Port Talbot who was also delayed, this time with a problem on the Severn Bridge.

Muttering that his punters were dropping like flies, he headed inside to do battle with the stuck door. He squirted some oil on the handle and jiggled in violently. The door remained firmly closed, but the handle sprayed the oil straight back in Dickie's face.

On the other side, Alan watched the handle violently yanked up and down and prayed the lock would hold.

Chapter 22

Charles was hungry. His unwanted stint of farm work had given him quite an appetite. And now he'd got Dickie's trousers and shoes on he decided it was safe to go and look for some food.

He pulled the attic door shut behind him and turned round to find himself face to face with a strange man wearing a pinafore. He blinked and then realised he was the guy who'd picked up the head of Ronald's doppelganger and then dropped it like a hot potato. Assuming he must be one of the caterers he said, 'I'm starving, so, what have you got for our lunch?'

'I haven't got time to talk about food; why aren't you dressed as a woman?'

'Because I'm now the Honourable Giles Forsythe.'

George could have screamed. 'No, no you've got to put the skirt and wig on again and pretend to be Caroline Timberlake.'

'What?' Charles had had enough of these endless script changes, who the hell was Caroline Timberlake - and why was the caterer telling him what to do? 'Where's Dickie.'

'I've no idea…but he told me to tell you.'

'Well, when you find him you can tell him nothing is going to make me put that skirt on again.' He tried to push past George, who refused to budge.

They stared at each other. George broke first. 'Look we're prepared to pay you if you dress up again.'

Charles was skint and Dickie had made it clear there would be no money until the weekend was over. Bizarre as the request sounded, perhaps he ought to hear what the man had to say. 'So, this is your idea not Dickie's.'

'No, well, yes.'

'Why?'

George flapped his hands around. 'It's too complicated to explain but all you have to do is pretend Mr Bishop is a real bishop and you're the new vicar called the Rev Caroline Timberlake. You won't have to keep the skirt on for long.

'What are you running here, some sort of kinky knocking shop for the clergy?'

'Certainly not,' but George could see that Charles was wavering. 'Look, we'll give you twenty pounds.' And he pulled two ten-pound notes out of his pocket and waved them under Charles' nose.

Charles carefully tested each note and tucked them into his trouser pocket, he could now afford the petrol home. 'Thanks.'

George felt his hopes rising. 'So, if you could go and get changed now.'

'Are you mad; nothing would get me into those clothes again,' and he pushed past George and headed towards the stairs, calling over his shoulder, 'but you can borrow them and act out any fantasy you want, they're in there in the attic.'

Never have hopes been dashed so quickly.

George rushed downstairs after him, but before he could catch up with him, Dickie grabbed him. 'The drawing room door's stuck again. Do you know what's the matter with it?

George tried to pull himself free 'It probably wants oiling.'

'I've tried that.' And he waved the oil can under George's nose.

'You know what these old properties are like it'll unstick itself in a minute.'

'I hope so otherwise I'll have to reconsider the fee I'm paying you.' He looked at George's pinnie. 'Have you finished doing the salad?'

'Nearly.'

'You need to start acting like a butler now so dump the pinnie. And where's Alan? Is he ready yet?'

'He's.... he's in the cloakroom.' A germ of an idea was creeping its way into George's brain, after all Charles had said he could borrow the clothes. 'I'll go and get his outfit.'

'By the way, he's a man.'

'I know he is.'

'I mean he's no longer playing a lady vicar. I've had to revise the script. So, he can wear his own clothes, he just needs a dog collar, it's in the attic.

'Oh, right, I'll just go and tell him.' And George headed towards the drawing room.

'I thought you said he was in the cloakroom.'

'Ah yes, so he is. I know, I'll pop upstairs and get the dog collar.'

'Well hurry up. The punters need to see a vicar and a butler.' Dickie was suspicious of George's fast disappearing back. But he was even more suspicious of Charles, who had just walked out of the kitchen carrying a plate.

'What the devil are you doing with those?' Dickie glared at the cheese sandwiches Charles was holding and didn't even notice Charles was wearing his shoes and trousers.

'I'm going to eat them - what do you think I'm going to do with them.'

Dickie snatched the plate away from him, 'No, you're not, you have to wait until all the guests have arrived.'

'But I'm hungry.'

'You should have had something before you got here.'

Charles decided to change the subject. 'You know you've got oil all over your face. You're never going to get away with being the maid looking like that,' And while Dickie rubbed his cheeks, spreading the oil even further, he snatched the plate again.

'So how would you like to be the maid,' Dickie hissed, 'after all you've got the right sort of voice now.'

'What are you talking about?'

'Well, you've had the snip, haven't you?'

'I've what?' Charles glared at Dickie.

'You don't have to pretend to me, I know all about it. You told everyone you'd had laryngitis so that no one would notice when your voice changed, right?'

'Who the hell told you that?'

'Ronald.'

'That lying bastard.' Charles was so angry he didn't notice his bread and cheese sliding off the plate onto the floor. 'I bloody well haven't had the snip.'

'So, you really did have laryngitis?'

'Yes, no…look, I pretended I couldn't speak to give me a reason for having a large scarf wrapped round my throat.'

'Why?'

Charles hesitated - it still wasn't something he was happy talking about. 'Because I had a big boil on my neck. You know what this profession's like, no one's going to give you a job if they think you're coming out in boils all the time.'

'Boils!' Dickie hurriedly stepped back in case they were catching. 'I hope they've gone now. We don't want to put the punters off.'

'It was only one and of course it's gone. You wait until I get hold of that bastard, I'm going to wring his bloody neck.'

'You haven't got time.'

Charles looked ready to argue, but at that moment Angela and Freda came down the stairs. Dickie immediately went in his maid mode. 'Ah Miss Andrews, Mrs Mortimer may I present the Honourable Giles Forsythe.'

Angela half curtsied. 'Oh, pleased to meet you, I'm sure.'

Freda didn't curtsey instead she glared at Charles and whispered. 'Careful Angela, he's the blackmailer.'

Before Angela could answer Charles had seized her hand and kissed it. 'Charmed Madam, charmed. Now if you'll excuse me, I have to finish my lunch.' And picking up some of the bread and cheese off the floor he walked up the stairs, leaving a pink-cheeked Angela gazing after him.

Freda sniffed. 'Pull yourself together Angela you're behaving like a teenager.' She turned to Dickie. 'We were looking for Mr Wilson.'

'He's a bit tied up at the moment can I help you.' Dickie was starting to think he was getting laryngitis, all this falsetto stuff was playing havoc with his throat.

'We need some brown paper and string.' Angela had resolutely refused to open her present and in the tussle with Freda the paper had got torn.

'I don't think he has any.'

'We'll have to buy our own then. Come along Angela.'

Dickie watched them put on their coats and go outside. 'They spend more time down the shops than they do here,' he muttered, picking up the rest of the bread and cheese and, blowing on them, he took them back into the kitchen.

Meanwhile in the attic Marigold slurped from her last bottle of gin, unaware that Ronald and Maddie had broken into the dining room cupboard housing her remaining bottles and were getting very tipsy on her precious booze.

Dickie's depleted troupe of actors had completely forgotten what they were in Kingsford for.

171

Chapter 23

The flyer looked as if it had been walked over by a dozen hikers in muddy books, but for some reason, which Jack Albright couldn't explain, he bent down and picked it up. He'd been standing nursing a hot coffee outside an all-night burger van in London wondering what to do next with his life, which included keeping it.

'You don't 'ave to 'ave that dirty old one, gov, I've got a 'ole pile here,' and the proprietor of 'Flaming Grills' pulled out a dozen from under the counter.

More as a distraction from his problems than any real interest Jack read it thoroughly. '"Murders 'R' Us"? What's that all about then, Maffia gone in for advertising?'' He held his mug up for a refill.

'Some artsy actor bloke dropped 'em off, Dickie someone, bit of a ginger.' When Jack didn't respond he added, 'You know a Perry Como.'

But Jack wasn't listening, he was thinking and he couldn't do both at the same time. A weekend in a Vicarage in the South West; no one would look for him there. And who knows what opportunities there might be. Rich blokes moving out of London for a bit of rural life, gullible farmers, wealthy widows; not to mention the people going for the weekend who must have a bob or two. And all of them wanting an original work of art, even if they didn't know it at the moment.

Because looking at him no one would believe he was a talented artist - he didn't fit the traditional view of a painter toiling over a canvas. That was because he didn't toil, he had the exceptional ability to be able to copy any of the great artists of the twentieth century and even some of the old masters. His particular favourite was Lowry and it was a Lowry which had caused the problem.

Unbeknown to Jack, the agent who handled his counterfeits, one Aubrey Wilcock, had sold a 'recently discovered' one to a collector who was as happy to keep his purchase hidden away as he was to keep his assets concealed from the Inland Revenue.

All would have been well if the collector, unable to resist the chance to gloat, hadn't shown it to a fellow patron of the arts who also collected Lowerys. Unfortunately, both had bought identical pictures. Denied the ability to go to the police the two collectors decided to collaborate in parting Aubrey from a section of his anatomy he was particularly fond of.

Jack could only hope that Aubrey had found a good place to hide because if he was found there was a strong possibility, if pressure was applied in certain tender areas, he would reveal the name of the forger.

He pulled out his mobile phone and dialled the number, hoping there was still a space for him.

Which was how he found himself bombing down the outside lane of the M4, heading for Kingsford in a Mercedes SL Roadster. He'd wanted a convertible but the hire company didn't have one.

Unable to have the top open he was forced to push his elbow out of his window as far as possible. It wasn't comfortable, but Jack was all about image. The fingers which rested lightly on the steering wheel were covered in heavy gold rings. He had several gold chain bracelets on his wrist and the obligatory gold medallion swinging in his open-neck shirt.

The wind might not be ruffling his hair, but there was quite a draught blowing round the back of his neck, which did not auger well.

With every passing mile Jack felt himself relaxing - Aubrey always sailed close to the wind, but always managed to steer clear of the rocks. His optimism took a dent when he hit the traffic jam several miles before Bristol. He looked in the rear-view mirror to check that the car behind him wasn't carrying four heavies bent on mischief. He caught the eye of an old lady, driving a Lada and winked at her.

But behind the bling and bravado, all Jack really wanted was the love of a good woman and a warm hearth to come home to.

Chapter 24

George knocked softly on the attic door. He was terrified of meeting Marigold in her underwear again, but he was even more terrified of what his wife would do if he hadn't paid the deposit.

But Marigold and Charles were sitting behind her screen eating the cheese sandwiches, after picking off the fluff, and swigging gin so George was able to slip in unnoticed. He saw the skirt, tights and jumper screwed up on one of the mattresses, so he screwed them up even more and pushed them into a carrier bag left on the floor next to a pair of high heeled shoes, which he also stuffed into the bag along with the wig.

In the drawing room Alan was pacing up and down and periodically checking on Herbert who was snoring and farting gently behind the sofa. It felt like hours since he had given George the money, but he was surprised to find, when he checked his watch, it was only a few minutes. He could feel his stress levels rising and he checked his pulse - it was banging up and down like a jack hammer.

When he heard a tap on the door he nearly jumped out of his skin. 'Who is it?' he whispered.

'It's me.'

'Who's me?'

'George, who do you think it is?'

Alan unlocked the door and George slipped inside and looked round the room. 'Where's the Bishop?'

'Asleep behind the sofa. I can't take much more of this.'

'You won't have to - as soon as he's had his talk with Caroline he'll be gone.' George pushed the carrier bag into Alan's hand. 'Now get changed before he wakes up.'

Alan pushed it back into George's hands. 'But I thought that Charles bloke was going to dress up and talk to the Bishop.'

George pushed it back to Alan. 'I can't find him. And Dickie wants you in your part straight away.'

Alan refused to take the bag. 'So, when's this Charles bloke going to talk to the Bishop?'

'He isn't. You are.'

'What! Oh no.'

'Look, it'll be easy; I mean you will be dressed for the part.'

'Are you mad?' And to emphasise the point he took the bag from George and threw it across the room scattering the contents.

George hurriedly picked them up. The tights now had a ladder and one sleeve of the jumper was pulling apart. 'It's our only chance. Think of Caroline, after all you will be doing it for her.'

Alan hesitated for one second then said, 'No, and if you couldn't find Charles, I'll have my money back.'

George hesitated for two seconds and then said, 'I…I had to give it to Dickie as a deposit for the clothes.'

'But I don't want them…,'

176

'So that's all the thanks I get for trying to cover up for Caroline and sort everything out.'

'...And I'm not wearing them.' Alan walked away and sat on the sofa so violently it shot backwards. There was a groan from behind.

Herbert had been enjoying a particularly pleasant dream where he was coxing the Oxford crew and they were winning the boat race by half a length when he was suddenly whacked in the face by an oar and tipped into the water.

Alan shot in the air like a particularly vigorous geyser.

George seized the initiative. 'We were so close to getting Caroline off the hook, but if you don't want to help her...,' He looked meaningfully at the sofa.

'All right, all right, I'll do it.' Alan snatched the clothes back.

'Hurry up then; go and get changed in the cloakroom.'

As soon as Alan left George peered over the back of the sofa. Herbert was sitting up and rubbing his eyes, one of which to George's horror was swelling up and turning multicoloured.

Even more worrying there was a large mirror over the fireplace. It was going to be difficult enough explaining how he came to be behind the sofa - a black eye would be impossible.

George pulled the sofa back and pulled Herbert to his feet. 'There you are My Lord, no harm done. Now shall we go and meet Caroline.'

'What was I doing, lying down there?' Herbert glared round the room and George quickly placed himself between Herbert and the mirror.

'I really couldn't say My Lord, I've only just found you like it.' And placing a firm hand on Herbert's back he pushed him towards the door. 'We don't want to keep the Vicar waiting, do we?'

But once in the hall it was clear that the Vicar was going to keep Herbert waiting because there was no sign of Alan. George cursed under his breath and guided Herbert round the room. 'Well, as you can see my Lord, the Vicarage has a very attractive hall with doors and a window...,'

Herbert wasn't interested in doors and windows and rudely cut in. 'I thought you said the Rev Timberlake was ready to see me.'

'She's just getting changed, she won't be long.' He pulled Herbert across to the hall table. 'And over here we have an interesting selection of hymn books and magazines....'

Luckily at that moment Alan appeared, tottering on the high heels, wig askew and with a large scarf he'd found hanging behind the cloakroom door wrapped round his face.

'Ah, here she is, at last My Lord.'

Herbert squinted at the blurry vision and headed towards it. 'Caroline, my dear, lovely to see you again.' He reached out to take Alan's hands, but Alan had hurriedly backed away nearly breaking his ankle as he struggled with the stilettos.

George stepped between them. 'Perhaps you shouldn't get too close my Lord in case you catch something. The Rev Timberlake has… a sore throat.'

'Yes, that's probably wise. After my little accident I wouldn't want to pick up a bug as well.' And he backed away as fast as Alan had.

Alan hissed at George, 'Why have you brought him out here?'

'Sorry, I didn't quite catch that.' Herbert leaned towards them.

'She says she's got a pain in her ear.' George turned and hissed at Alan, 'I had to bring him out, there's a mirror in there.'

'So, what was it going to do, fall on his head?'

'Pardon, I can't hear you.'

George shouted over his shoulder, 'She says she's pleased to meet you, but her eyes have gone red.'

'If only she'd speak up a bit, I wouldn't need an interpreter.' Herbert was getting irritable.

George hissed, 'No, but he would have seen his black eye, how was I going to explain that Alan?'

Alan looked round nervously, 'Well, we can't stay here, supposing someone comes.'

'I didn't quite catch that.'

'Sorry My Lord, she says she's got the runs.'

'This is ridiculous. I want us all to sit down, somewhere comfortable and have an informal chat about the way forward for women. And where's the other Church Warden? Go and get him.'

'I can't.'

179

'What! Are you disobeying your Bishop?'

'I...I can't leave the vicar My Lord. You won't understand what she's saying.'

'Oh, for goodness sake, I didn't come all this way just to say hello and goodbye. Look, my dear go and take an aspirin or something for your throat and then we can have a chat.' Herbert folded his arms and started tapping his foot.

Alan hissed at George, 'You'll have to take over as the vicar. I'll go and get changed.'

'What did she say?'

'She said she's mentally deranged.' George choked as Alan grabbed him round the throat. 'Sorry, I misheard, she wants to get changed.' He pulled Alan's hands away and hissed back, 'Don't you dare take those clothes off.'

Herbert tapped his foot even faster and a vein throbbed in tune near his black eye. 'Well, if she thinks a new outfit will make her feel better so be it, but tell her to hurry up.'

'Thank you, sir,' and Alan rushed back to the cloakroom, but before George could haul him back Dickie came out or the kitchen and held on to his arm.

'Ah George, I'm still missing one vicar.' Then catching sight of Herbert, he added, 'What's he doing back here I thought you'd got rid of him.'

'I'm just about to.'

Forgetting he was supposed to be the maid, Dickie walked across, seized Herbert's hand and shook it hard. 'Well, nice to meet you again, old love. I hope all your troubles will soon be over.'

Herbert blinked suspiciously at the cheeky maid's outfit and Dickie's oil-stained cheeks, this wasn't Caroline, it was a man in drag. But a short stint of being a vicar in San Francisco stood him in good stead and he managed to mutter, 'How kind, how kind.'

'Can I see you in the kitchen again, George? A small matter of lunch, Charles has taken half it... oh and the two sisters have gone shopping again.'

'Yes, in a moment, but you want me to get rid of him, first don't you?'

'Well, make it snappy, and then you'd better think about what we are going to do for food, because I don't think your caterers are coming,' and Dickie ducked back into the kitchen.

In the cloakroom. Alan kicked off the shoes and sighed with relief, but he still had to struggle out of the tights which now had even more ladders in them. He wanted to throw the whole lot out of the window, but old habits die hard and he neatly folded each garment and laid it on the toilet seat with the shoes side by side next to the toilet brush holder. He wondered what to do with the wig and eventually hung it on a hook behind the door along with the scarf.

Straightening his tie, he walked into the hall to see an angry George pacing up and down. Smirking at the thought of George wearing the high heels and wig he ignored his fellow church warden and walked across to Herbert. 'You wanted to see me, sir?'

'Yes, but where's the Rev Timberlake? I can't hang about here all day.' Herbert was getting seriously worried that his wife might have returned home to the palace early and would come looking for him.

'Perhaps Mr Williams ought to go and look for her.' Alan smirked at George.

Herbert glared at George. 'Well don't just stand there, go and find her.'

A furious George headed for the cloakroom hissing at Alan as he passed, 'I'll get you for this.'

Alan knew it would take George several long minutes to get changed. The outfit had been tight on him and George was even bigger. He couldn't risk taking Herbert back into the drawing room and when he tried the dining room handle the door wouldn't open.

'Sorry, I think the door lock needs oiling.' He guided Herbert to the hall table. 'Umm, have you seen our hymn books?'

'Yes, and the magazines, and the front door and windows.' Herbert tried to squint at his watch. 'How much longer is she going to be? Surely he's found her by now.'

'You're absolutely right, sir. Perhaps I'd better go and look for them.' He headed towards the cloakroom.

'Now they've all disappeared. What is this place, the Marie Celeste?'

He spun round hopefully when the front door opened, but it was only two elderly women whom he vaguely recognised from somewhere.

Chapter 25

'Henrietta? It's Flora here.'

Herbert was right to worry, his wife *had* come home early. Heading for Midsomer Norton to open the Mother's Union annual bring and buy sale she'd got caught up in the diversions which sent drivers in every direction but the right one. As her return meant missing luncheon with the MU President she arrived back at the palace in a cold fury – and her fury got even colder when she found the palace not only empty of her husband but his Rover as well. Putting two and two together, she quickly realised that these events were not unconnected.

Herbert had gone awol and she had a pretty shrewd idea where he might have gone. But how had he done it? She checked her handbag and both sets of car keys were still in there. And they had never left her sight long enough for him to get a new set cut. Also why was there a tennis ball with a slit in it, an odd-looking pair of clippers and a roll of duct tape on the garage floor.

It was a puzzle but she didn't have time to think about it at the moment. Because of the traffic she knew she would never get to Kingsford in less than three hours so there was only one thing to do - ring Lady Henrietta of Kingsford Manor.

The two had been gels together at a Swiss finishing school where they had learned basic French, how to make a cheese fondue and the ten rules for keeping husbands in check.

'Herbert's gone off, despite my clearest instructions, and I think he's visiting that new vicar in your church.'

Henrietta didn't actually own the church, although through some quaint medieval quirk she had a say in who was given the living. Flora had hoped she would be an ally in stopping Caroline being selected, but for once Herbert had got his way and Flora had not entirely forgiven Henrietta - and now held her responsible.

'So?' Henrietta had enough problems with her own husband Selwyn, an inveterate gambler and idiot.

'So, I want you to go straight round there and tell him to come home at once.'

'Why don't you ring the Vicarage and tell him yourself?'

Flora didn't want to admit that she was refusing to speak to Caroline. It wasn't the girl's fault of course, but a stand had to be taken. She was also hesitant to admit that Herbert might ignore her demand to return home. So, a more subtle move had to be made, 'I could Henrietta of course I could, very easily, but he has such respect for you and you have a way of handling him…so much better than I have.'

Henrietta snorted, she didn't believe a word Flora said, but she couldn't refuse to help a fellow pupil. Men, in her experience, were as slippery as a tinned sardine - a fish she was well acquainted with as it formed a staple part of Kingsford Manor lunches.

'I will do what I can Flora, but he has got a bit bolshie lately. I think you've been too lenient with him. Remember what Mademoiselle Éclair used to tell us, '*Ne laissez pas un mari prendre un pouce ou il prendra un mile*".'

Flora thought was easy for Mlle Éclair to talk about not giving an inch, she'd never been married. 'Well, do your best Henrietta.' She sighed deeply, 'I think he's going through a mid-life crisis.'

'Don't be ridiculous, Flora, you are both well past middle age. No, this is civil disobedience and you have to nip it in the bud.'

Chapter 26

Freda and Angela had been hoping to creep in unnoticed with their roll of brown paper, but Herbert was standing in the hall in their way. Hiding herself behind Freda, Angela whispered, 'There's that farmer person.'

Freda, using her best headmistress voice said, 'What are you doing in here, my man?'

'Trying to tend my flock, although they keep disappearing.'

'Well, you won't find any sheep in here.'

'Mr Wilson said we should push him out if we saw him in here again Freda.'

Freda nodded. 'I think it's high time you popped off home.' And seizing Herbert in a grip of iron she frogmarched him to the front door.

'Take your hands off me Madam don't you know who I am?'

'Of course we do,' said Angela quickly opening the front door for Freda to push him through.

From outside there was a loud bang, a long wail and then silence.

Angela looked worried. 'I said the path was slippery after that shower. Do you think we ought to go and help him?'

Freda glanced out of the window. 'No, it's alright, he's wandered off. Right, let's get that gun wrapped up.'

186

But before they could escape upstairs George wobbled out of the cloakroom, supported by Alan, and glared at them. 'Where's the Bishop?'

Freda glared right back at him, was it the same female vicar as before? It was difficult to tell with all that hair over her face. 'Are you the Vicar?'

'Yes, now where's the Bishop?'

'We were told the vicar was a man now.'

Not to be outdone Angela added. 'Mr Wilson said the Bishop had defrocked you.'

'Yes, well, I put it back on again.' The tights were squeezing George in places he preferred to not to be squeezed in and it was making him waspish. 'Now, where is he?'

'Do you mean the real Bishop?'

'Yes.'

'The last time I saw him Mrs Forbes was taking him into the dining room.'

Alan groaned. 'Not again, now what are we going to do?'

'This is all your fault, Alan, why did you leave him on his own.'

'Because you were taking too long getting your tights on.'

'I was managing just fine until you burst in and yanked them up.' George saw the two women staring at him open-mouthed. 'Well, I was.' And with a defiant hitch to his skirt, he staggered across to the dining room door and tried the handle – several times.

'It's locked.' He placed an ear against the door panel.

Alan joined him. 'What's she doing to him?'

'Well, they're not singing hymns that's for sure.' George wobbled up and down the hall. 'We've got to get him out of there.' He glared at Alan, 'Have you got any bright ideas.'

But Alan was out of ideas, bright or otherwise.

George was getting desperate. 'All we want is a quick chat with him and then we can get rid of him, for good.'

Angela whispered, 'Freda, they're going to kill the Bishop. What are we going to do?'

'We must hurry up and post this gun to the police, and we'll add that to the anonymous note.' And hoping Alan and George weren't following them, they quickly made their way up to their bedroom.

But George and Alan had already gone into the drawing room to listen through the wall.

Chapter 27

Tom and Edna finally came to a stop on the M5 after crawling along at two miles an hour for what seemed a life time. They had left Dulverton in plenty of time to get to Kingsford Vicarage for coffee and now it looked as if they wouldn't even make it for lunch.

Edna wasn't worried about food; she had enough provisions packed in the boot to feed a three-man assault on Everest. Although the murder mystery weekend was all inclusive, she didn't want her husband to go hungry so she'd packed a large fruit cake, three different quiches, six rounds of corned beef sandwiches, half a dozen hard-boiled eggs and two giant-size packets of crisps as well as a variety of fruits, salads, two flasks of coffee and two bottles of wine.

The recipient of this largess was staring moodily at the stationary line of traffic in front of him. Police sergeant Tom Cowden, recently retired, didn't want to miss one minute of the weekend. Ever since he joined the Force straight from school, he had been desperate to become a detective and solve murders, but it had never happened. So, to compensate, his former colleagues presented him with a brochure for a 'Murders 'R' Us' weekend and a voucher entitling him and his wife to take part in two exciting days, solving a heinous crime involving 'jealousy, passion and murder most foul'. And Tom was taking it very seriously.

He glanced over his shoulder to check that his briefcase was still sitting on the backseat. It contained a note book, a finger-printing outfit, some plaster of Paris powder for taking casts of footprints, a book on the psychological profiling of psychopaths and another on the body language of the guilty. On top was a polaroid a camera to photograph the suspects, as well as the corpse, and a small tape recorder. And tucked into the footwell was a large white board and marker pen.

Edna patted his knee. 'Now, don't you fret dear, it won't have started yet.'

'I just want to get there, get a feel of the place, first impressions are very important in a murder inquiry.'

'I don't suppose anyone has been murdered yet.'

But Tom was not to be mollified. He peered through the windscreen and could just make out that the traffic on the bridges crossing the motorway was also at a standstill. In one decisive movement he pulled onto the hard shoulder, completely forgetting he was no longer a serving police officer, and drove towards the turn-off for Weston-super-mare.

The other motorists glared at him as he rumbled past them. None of them had the nerve to follow him but each driver edged forward as close as possible to the car in front, determined that they weren't going to be the one to let him back in to the queue.

Just before the slip road, which was completely blocked, Tom came to a halt and told Edna that to be on the safe side she should get out of the car and stand well away it from while he sorted out the situation.

'Don't be daft Tom, I don't think anyone is going to drive into me, nothing's moving. No, no, I'll be quite safe in here.' She almost added that she was probably in more danger from the angry drivers glaring at them than an errant lorry barrelling down the hard shoulder.

She watched the tall figure of her husband walk up between the cars and disappear from view. Perhaps she had time to get one of the flasks out of the boot and a chocolate biscuit.

If the glares of the other motorists had been icy before it was nothing to what they were now when they saw Edna enjoying a steaming cup of coffee and a Kit Kat. She locked all the doors and looked resolutely ahead.

Tom quickly assessed the situation; he hadn't been commended for handling traffic congestion for nothing. The traffic lights were still turning green in rotation, but even though the roundabout was gridlocked drivers still tried to edge forward when the lights were in their favour, adding to the chaos.

Tom walked across to a young, uniformed constable trying unsuccessfully to unravel the knotted streams of cars, buses, lorries, coaches and a horse box, whose cargo was kicking hell out of the flooring.

'Alright son I'll give you hand.'

'I'm sorry sir, but members of the public aren't allowed to direct traffic.' The constable felt seriously worried, supposing all the drivers got out of their cars and started interfering. He had visions of a mass brawl.

'I'm police sergeant Tom Cowden and I'm on my way to solve a murder Constable, so I need to get to Kingsford Vicarage asap.'

The constable felt a weight lifting off his shoulders, the sergeant outranked him so let him sort it out. 'Am I glad to see you sir they won't take no notice of me.'

Tom wasn't surprised the lad only looked about fourteen. 'Stand in front of that car over there and don't let it move.' He then crossed to the next lane and pointed an authoritative finger at a bullish man in a beaten-up Jeep who was completely blocking the junction. 'Back up please sir.'

The driver looked as if he was about to refuse, but Tom's digit was not to be argued with so he inched back as far as he could, forcing the car behind to do the same. Slowly Tom cleared a gap and gradually the chaos began to untangle.

'You should be alright now son.' And without a backward glance at the grateful constable, he strode down the slip road, which was now moving freely, and got back into his car. But it then took him fifteen minutes before anyone would let him back in to the queue on the slip road.

'They don't deserve you,' said Edna as they headed up the A370. She popped a chocolate lime sweet in his mouth, 'selfish whatnots.'

Later than night in bed, drinking the coco his mother had brought up to him, the young constable thought about Sergeant Cowden. Should he have asked to see his warrant card? He took another sip, no that would have

192

been rude and the guy did know what he was doing so must have been trained in traffic duty. But as he was snuggling down under his Star Wars-patterned duvet another thought hit him, wasn't it detectives who solved murders, not plain sergeants?

Chapter 28

After finishing the cheese sandwiches and emptying the gin bottle, Charles and Marigold were still sitting companionably behind her screen gossiping about actors they knew when Charles said 'Well this weekend's turning out to be a bit of a cock up isn't it?'

Marigold gave a slight shiver. 'That reminds me Charles, I just want to say I think what you've done is wonderful.'

'What, playing the part of Giles?'

'No, you know…when you pretended to have laryngitis.'

'Well, it may not have been laryngitis but I can tell you, it was bloody painful.'

Marigold clutched her chest. 'Oh, I bet it was. Did you have a general or a local anaesthetic?'

Charles looked at her in amazement. 'Anaesthetic! No, I didn't have anything.'

Marigold clutched her chest even tighter. 'Nothing! But didn't it hurt?'

'Too bloody right it did.'

'But that's appalling. Where did you go to have it done?'

'Nowhere, I did it myself.'

Marigold could hardly speak. 'You did it yourself! Couldn't you afford to have it done properly?'

'I didn't want anyone to see it, it was so large.'

Marigold felt her temperature rising, 'Oh my word,' she gasped, fanning herself violently. 'So, what did you do?'

'Well, I cauterised a knife on the gas stove and pierced it.'

'I think I'm going to faint.'

'I damn nearly fainted myself. But it did the trick. And it hardly left a scar, do you want to see?'

Marigold peered round the blanket to check they were still alone, 'Well, if you're sure.'

'Look.'

Marigold hurriedly stood up and walked away, the last thing she wanted to see was the nasty scar on his neck where he'd pulled his collar down. 'What are you talking about? I thought you'd had a vasectomy.'

'A vasectomy! No, I had a boil. That bloody Ronald, I'm going to kill him when I find him.'

'So am I.' Disappointment always made Marigold feel vicious.

In their bedroom, Freda and Angela were struggling to wrap up the gun. However much wrapping paper they put round it, it still looked like a gun, only bigger. They had tried hiding it under one of the bedside rugs, but the bulge was unmistakeable so they had to get rid of it.

'Supposing the postman accidently presses the trigger, someone could be hurt Freda.'

Freda snatched up her pen and started writing on it, FRAGILE HANDLE WITH CARE. Then she saw that Angela had written her name and address on the back.

'What did you do that for?'

'You're supposed to write it on the outside of a parcel, in case the Post Office has to return it.'

'We don't want it returned you ninny.' Exasperated, Freda tore off the paper and started wrapping it again. They were quickly getting through their roll of paper and cellotape.

But Angela now has something else to worry about. 'What if the Post Mistress asks us what it is? Don't they have a list of things you can't send through the post?'

'Well, we're not going to tell her it's a gun are we.' Freda looked at the parcel. 'We'll say it's a banana.'

Chapter 29

Charles, with Marigold hard on his heels, ran down the stairs to the hall. Marigold pointed to the dining room door 'Let's look in there first.'

'Right let's get this so-called bishop.' He pressed an ear against the door and could vaguely hear hiccupping. 'Yes, he's in there I recognise his belch.' When he found the door was locked, he started hammering on it. 'Come out you bastard this time I'm really am going to kill him.'

The commotion had brought George and Alan out of the drawing room. George grabbed Charles' arm 'What's the matter with you, you've already hit him once, why do you want to kill him?'

'He's been telling everyone I've had a vasectomy.'

'What, the Bishop?' Alan grabbed his other arm and between them they managed to drag him away from the door.

'Yes, the bloody bishop.'

Marigold, who hadn't forgotten George's rebuff of her charms earlier, not to mention bursting into the attic when she was *en dishabille*, waded into the furore and tried to pull George away from Charles all the while screaming at the top of her voice like a banshee.

Upstairs Angela struggled to push the chest of drawers up against their bedroom door. 'It's that mad woman, Freda, I can hear her screaming.'

'No, we have to get rid of the gun.'

Charles pulled himself free. 'This is between him and me.' And before anyone could stop him, he flung himself against the door and bounced straight back off.

On the other side of the door Ronald, who had drunk half a bottle of Bols gin was now full of Dutch courage. Despite swaying on his feet, his fists were up and he was ready to rumble. 'Open the door dear lady and let me at him.'

But it was the front door swinging dramatically open which caused four heads to swivel round and stare, mesmerised, at Bishop Herbert swaying precariously in the entrance. So, Ronald and Maddie's grand entrance fell rather flat.

Maddie was the first to break the silence. 'Oh look, there's the other bishop.'

'So, you're the impostor,' Ronald roared and pulling back his fist he caught Herbert full in the left eye. Luckily George was once more able to catch him and lower him gently to the floor.

Ronald raised his arms like a prize fighter and took a bow. A fatal mistake as Charles, who now had his glasses back and could see exactly what he was doing, launched a quick upper cut, catching him full in his right eye. 'Take that you bastard.'

Ronald dropped like a stone, but no one thought to catch him and lower him gently to the ground.

At the top of the stairs Angela and Freda stood frozen in horror. Their desperation to get rid of the gun had overcome their fear of leaving their room and now they were wishing they hadn't.

'Oh Freda, they're at it again.'

'Try to act naturally, Angela, and just ignore them.'

In the kitchen Dickie, who'd been desperately going through cupboards and the refrigerator in the hopes that he had overlooked something edible, once again heard the unmistakeable sound of brawling. By the time he reached the hall the worst was over.

Quickly assessing the situation Dickie looked up. 'Ah, Miss Andrews, Mrs Mortimer, sorry there seems to have been another little accident.'

'Has there, we hadn't notice anything had we Angela?'

'No, nothing, nothing at all.' And she followed her sister who was stepping over the two bodies and heading for the front door.

Marigold glared at them. 'Are both you mad?'

Freda swung round slowly, the gun-shaped parcel under her arm pointing straight at Marigold's chest and gave her the full 'what little turd are you to speak to a head mistress like that' stare.

Marigold, not to be outdone, gave Freda her best 'Dame Sybil Thorndyke in The Importance of Being Ernest' stare.

Dickie, sensing the staring competition might soon escalate said, 'This is Lady Alicia, ladies.'

Angela immediately dropped into a half curtsey, not easy with her feet either side of an unconscious man. 'Oh, Your Ladyship.'

Freda sniffed. 'Lady Alicia indeed. You're no better than you ought to be. Having a bath with your butler, I've never heard anything like it.'

Maddie who had grown tired of being a bystander in all the excitement, turned to Charles. 'So, who are you then?'

'The Honourable Giles Forsythe, madam,' and he kissed her hand.

'Oh, yes, I've heard about you. Shall we go into the drawing room and get to know each other better?'

Freda swung the parcel in Maddie's direction, 'Have you no shame woman, he's Lady Alicia's lover.'

Maddie wiggled her fingers, 'Not any more,' and she pulled Charles into the drawing room.

As soon as Charles was safely out the way Ronald sat up, clutching his eye. 'What hit me?'

'Charles did and it serves you right, spreading gossip about him.' Marigold was tired of trying to outstare Freda so vented her spleen on Ronald.

Knowing he could rely on Maddie to keep Charles busy until he calmed down, Ronald said, 'I think I'll just pop upstairs and bathe my eye.' He staggered to his feet and, stepping over Herbert, headed to the bathroom. Marigold who was determined to give him a good tongue lashing was hard on his heels.

George took off his wig and looked at the recumbent Herbert. 'I can't cope with much more.'

Angela started at him, 'You're not the vicar, you're the butler.'

'Not even close, I'm the Church Warden.'

'Good heavens! That's even worse, what were you doing scrubbing Lady Alicia's back?' Freda was outraged.

Herbert groaned and held his head, 'Pardon?'

Freda bent over and shouted at him, 'Lady Alicia's back.'

'Is she! Where's she been then?'

Alan knelt down and started rubbing Herbert's hands. 'I think he's hallucinating.'

George knelt down on the other side of Herbert and waved his hand in front of the Bishop's face. 'Do you know who you are?'

Herbert struggled to focus on the hand. Was it his? If it was it seemed to have a mind of its own because it started slapping his face. 'No do you?'

Freda decided it was a good time to leave, the front door was still open and she wanted to get through it. 'Yes, well we've got to get going, come along Angela.'

Dickie, once again forced his voice up an octave, 'But we can't let you leave now, can we George? We're only just getting started.' He quickly shut the front door and stood in front of it.

Angela felt her knees buckle, things were worse than ever, now they were going to be held prisoner. 'But we've got to get to the Post Office,' she squeaked.

Dickie reached for the parcel, 'George can take that down for you later.' But before he could touch it Freda had assumed the braced stance of a CIA agent and was holding the parcel out in front of her with both hands firmly clasped round one end.

'Stand back, this parcel is loaded.' She'd never done anything like this before and a frisson of excitement swept through her body.

Next to her Angela shouted, 'Let'm have it, Freda,' and glared round the hall.

The silence stretched out - even when the phone rang nobody moved, no one said a word, but six pairs of eyes flickered towards it.

Then a voice from the floor said, 'I've got a funny ringing sound in my head.'

George stood up and, stepping over Herbert, grabbed the phone. 'Hello...', then through gritted teeth he added, 'yes dear, I will even if it kills me.' He slammed the receiver back down.

Angela grabbed Fred's arm, 'Oh Freda, now the church warden's going to be killed.'

Freda shook her off and waved the parcel from side to side. 'Don't anyone move. We know all about what's going on here, oh yes. Robbery, blackmail...'

'...and sex. Don't forget the sex, Freda.'

'Yes, alright Angela, I was coming to the sex. Robbery, blackmail, sex...and one of you is a killer.'

Dickie was very impressed. In all the years he'd been doing his murder mysteries none of the punters had ever got so caught up in the action. 'Well, you two really are getting into the spirit of things, aren't you?' He reached for the parcel - it was now time to calm things down a bit.

But Freda wasn't going to give it up. 'I warned you to stay back.' She squeezed the parcel and from inside came a small bang like the sound from a cap gun.

Angela screamed and Freda dropped the parcel on Dickie's foot. He picked it up and pulled off the paper. 'So that's where the gun got to. Thank you, ladies, we need this for tomorrow's murder.'

'Tomorrow's murder?' Angela again clutched Freda's arm and this time Freda didn't shake her off.

'Yes, there's going to be lots of blood everywhere.'

'Freda, it's Psycho all over again.'

'Whatever you do, don't go in the shower, Angela.' And she pulled her sister upstairs at a run with Dickie in hot pursuit, waving the gun.

'But it wouldn't be any fun if we didn't have a corpse.' He knocked on their bedroom door, but all he could hear was the sound of furniture being dragged across the room.

Marigold, who was standing outside the bathroom shouting at Ronald through the door, walked along the landing and listened with him. 'What the hell are they doing in there?'

Dickie shrugged, 'Moving furniture for some reason.'

Chapter 30

Herbert finally managed to get himself up by pulling on George's legs. 'Why was that woman waving a gun about?'

'Because she's a homicidal maniac.'

'Oh, right…lives here does she?'

George hung onto the wavering Bishop and whispered to Alan, 'That's lucky, I think he's lost his memory.'

'Do you think he's forgotten all about wanting to see Caroline?'

'I'll ask him. Do you know why you're here, My Lord?'

'No, haven't a clue, do you?'

Alan felt a brief surge of happiness. 'Oh, that's wonderful, he's completely flipped.'

'Quick, run him back to the Palace before he remembers anything.' He pulled Herbert towards the front door, 'Come along, My Lord, this way, Mr Palmer's going to take you home,' and he thrust him into Alan's arms.

Alan pushed him back into George's arms, 'How am I supposed to drive him home, Mother's got the car.'

'Use his of course.'

'And how am I going to get back from the palace…and don't say walk.'

'I'll come and pick you up as soon as I have got rid of everyone,' and he pushed Herbert back into Alan's arms.

'You'd better.'

'Yes, I'm feeling much better, thank you.' Herbert was struggling to follow the conversation and couldn't understand why two men seemed to be fighting over him.

No sooner had George shut the door behind the pair than Dickie came bouncing back down the stairs.

'I don't know what we are going to do about those two old dears. I think they've barricaded themselves in their bedroom. Still, I expect they'll come out when they're hungry.' He stared at George's legs with their laddered tights, with the crotch now hanging well below his skirt, 'By the way, why are you dressed as the lady vicar, I thought Alan was taking that part. Not that he has to be a woman anymore.'

'Ahhhh…yes, well, you see…he's gone. He refused to have anything to do with it so I decided to take on both roles to help you out. So, if I could just have my money….'

Outside Alan had a sense of déjà vu as he tried to manhandle the bishop down the steps. Was it less than an hour or so ago he'd done the very same thing for that actor? Then it hit him, in all the pandemonium he'd completely forgotten he'd locked the guy in his bathroom. Well, he'd obviously managed to escape and get back to the Vicarage. Alan hoped it was before his mother got back from her drive.

But now he had something else to worry about, 'Which is your car, sir?'

Herbert looked blearily round the gravel drive. He didn't think it was the Reliant Robin. Then he spotted it – an open top Morgan. The memories came flooding back of his carefree youth, roaring round the South Downs, a beautiful young lady at his side screaming with excitement. He couldn't remember her name but it wasn't Flora. 'It's this one.'

Alan stared at the low-slung sports car and then at the bishop. How on earth was he going to get him into that. He wasn't entirely sure he could get himself into it. 'Are you sure this is yours? Shouldn't we look for another one?'

Herbert glared at him belligerently, he wanted the Morgan. 'No, I want this one,' and showing a niftiness that belied his years not to mention his two black eyes and the lump on his head, he climbed over the door into the driver's seat.

Unconsciously parodying his mother Alan said primly, 'I want doesn't get.' Then he remembered he was talking to the Bishop. 'I'll just keep looking, sir.' He saw a maroon Rover tucked close to the hedge, the personalised number plate said 1 BIS H. He glanced back at Herbert who was making car noises and rocking the steering wheel violently from side to side.

'Could you give me your car keys sir.' Alan hoped that if he got the Rover started the bishop might be more amenable to getting in it.

Herbert glared at him. He hated having his daydream spoilt and he was still trying to remember the name of the young lady. He felt in his pocket. 'I haven't got any.'

'But you must have.' Alan had another sense of déjà vu, that actor bloke hadn't had any keys on him either. 'Did you leave them in the attic?'

'No of course I didn't.' Herbert wracked his brains, he vaguely remembered using a tennis ball and tinkering with a steering column. Was that this morning or last week, 'No, I hotwired it, didn't need a key,' and he went back rocking the steering wheel and living the dream.

Alan was getting desperate - he didn't believe a word about the hotwiring but he could hardly insist on searching the bishop's pockets. His only hope was that the keys had fallen out somewhere in the Vicarage.

George had followed Dickie into the kitchen. 'I really do need to take the money to the Post Office to pay it into the church accounts.' He looked at this watch, the deadline for paying the caterers their deposit was fast approaching and he had a twenty-minute drive to get to their office.

If he hadn't left it so late, he could have sent a cheque, but now they wanted cash. He was beginning to think membership of an exclusive golf club wasn't worth the anguish he was going through, especially as he hadn't even had time to swing a club there let alone play a round. One thing was certain, he couldn't go home until he paid the money or died in the attempt and the latter was looking the more likely.

Instead of answering him Dickie pulled open all the cupboards and the 'fridge. 'As you can see old love the cupboards are bare and there's still no sign of the caterers.' He slammed them all shut, 'So until I know that I can give the punters their lunch, for which they have paid, there's no money for you.'

'I told you I rang and they'd definitely left.'

'But they haven't arrived and that's what counts.'

'What if I was to run down to the Post Office and buy some bread and cheese, they sell lovely locally-made bread in there. Or even better you could drive me down.'

'I can't leave my guests unattended.' What he actually meant was he couldn't risk leaving Ronald, Charles and Marigold to their own devices. He looked at George and decided it was a safe bet he would come back and not scuttle off home. 'No, you'll have to go on foot.'

'But I'll need some money.'

Dickie sighed, pulled out a wallet and carefully counted out three ten-pound notes, 'And I shall expect some change.'

For a fleeting second George was tempted to snatch the bulging wallet and run for it. Instead, he took the notes and headed out the back door. To his surprise, he was still clutching the blonde wig so he threw it under a bush.

At the very same moment as Alan came in the front door.

Chapter 31

Alan quickly looked round the hall, but couldn't see any car keys. He tried to remember which rooms the bishop had been in. He really hoped the keys weren't in that Maddie woman's bed. He'd leave that one until last.

He headed to the drawing room, more in hope than certainty - and he was right to be uncertain. After pulling out the sofa, lifting the carpets and checking behind the curtains it was clear that the Bishop's car keys were not there. He headed for the library with even less belief he would find them. A quick glance out of the window, confirming Herbert was still trying to remove the steering wheel from the Morgan, leant his search an air of desperation. Whoever owned that car was not going to be happy.

He searched the room from top to bottom, even pushing his fingers down the side of the arm chairs – nothing. The dining room door was still closed and he could hear Maddie and Charles chatting in there. If he was quick, he could search her room while it was empty.

Feeling hot under the collar he pulled back her duvet and checked under the pillows, averting his eyes from the lacy nightie which had been tucked under them. It was only his love for Caroline which kept him going.

After groping under the bed, where a pair of fluffy slippers proved empty of keys, he knew it was hopeless.

As George disappeared out the back door Dickie wondered if he should have reminded him that he was still dressed as a lady vicar, but then decided George would probably notice that himself before he got far.

After checking his souffle was setting he crossed to the dining room to lay the table for lunch, hoping more food would be turning up from somewhere. Maddie and Charles were sitting chatting and he noticed another empty gin bottle had been added to the collection on the table.

'Sorry, ma'am, sir, I need to lay the table,' and he gave a quick bob.

Maddie stood up and said she would go upstairs to get ready for lunch. As soon as she'd gone Dickie told Charles to go and mingle.

'Who with?'

Dickie was about to say the guests when he remembered only three had arrived so far and two of those had barricaded themselves in their room. 'Alright, go and apologise to Ronald.'

Charles nodded, but he had no intention of doing that. Instead, bolstered by half a bottle of Bols, he was going to retrieve his suitcase, but first he had a pressing need. 'I just need to go to the cloakroom first.'

Once in there he was surprised to find a pile of men's clothes thrown on the floor. Then, checking that Dickie was still busy searching for cutlery in the enormous Victorian sideboard, he slipped out the front door.

He noticed the farmer who'd been punched by Ronald, sitting in Dickie's Morgan and gave him a cheery wave before setting off down the road.

When she got to her room, Maddie noticed her wardrobe was swaying slightly, but put it down to the gin and decided to lay on the bed for a few moments until it stayed still.

Inside Alan stood petrified pressed up against her heavily scented dresses, desperately trying not to sneeze as her perfume hit the back of his nose.

After laying the table Dickie noticed his oil can still sitting on the hall table and decided to put it back in his car.

He was not best pleased to see Herbert sitting in the Morgan trying to wrench the steering wheel off its column. Muttering under his breath about bloody farmers he unlocked the driver's door, pulled the unfortunate Bishop out and dragged him into the road. Giving him a sharp push, he told him to clear off and not come back.

He waited until Herbert had disappeared into a ditch and then went back to the Morgan to see if any damage had been done. The steering felt decidedly slack so he drove it round the back of the Vicarage out of harm's way and parked it on the gravel terrace outside the kitchen door, where he could keep an eye on it. Then he locked the back door.

George was taking a short cut across the playing fields before he remembered he was trying to run in a skirt and high heels. He ground to a halt in despair – should he go back to the Vicarage and change or carry on to his house and change. The latter course would only work if he could avoid his wife which was unlikely.

As he dithered, he saw a lone child on a swing that he vaguely recognised as belonging to the Sunday school. Snapping the heels of his shoes he staggered across and offered the young lad a ten-pound note to buy a loaf of bread, a slab of cheese, a carton of butter and some sweets for himself.

When young Simon presented himself at the Post Office with the money, and a tale that the Church Warden, dressed as a woman, had given it to him he was roundly condemned as a story-teller by most of the villagers – but not all. The Post Mistress concluded he must have found the note and just made the story up so she put the money in the charity box. Those who thought Simon was telling the truth about the cross-dressing Church Warden muttered to each other they'd seen this coming for a long time. Meanwhile the Post Mistress made more coffee for the onlookers who declared the morning's entertainment was getting better and better, and Simon's tears were assuaged by a lollypop.

Chapter 32

Charles was feeling almost happy. His knuckles stung a bit, but giving Ronald a black eye was worth a bit of pain. He strode down the road towards the farm enjoying the sun and looking neither left nor right - so missed an arm sticking out of the ditch, trying to get a grip on a clump of Cow Parsley.

But while he didn't notice Herbert struggling to pull himself out of the mud, he certainly noticed his car was no longer in the farmyard. He inched his way round the edge of the cow dung to the front door and hammered on it. After ten minutes he heard chains and bolts being slid back and the door opened to reveal a vision.

In a nanosecond Charles had taken in the sparkling green eyes, creamy skin and plaited auburn hair atop a slender figure dressed in a white t-shirt and blue dungarees.

The vision spoke, 'Sorry it took me so long to answer the door, most people come round the back and walk straight in.' She waited for him to speak, but when the silence dragged on, she folded her arms, put her head on one side and viewed him suspiciously. 'Can I help you?'

Charles recovered his power of speech, 'I've come to get my suitcase, but my car's gone.'

The vision laughed and pulled him through the door into the hallway. 'You must be the guy that ran out of petrol. Sorry about my dad, he's got a weird sense of humour.'

Weird was not a strong enough word in Charles' mind, but he wasn't going to say anything against his future father-in-law. Although the vision didn't yet know it, they were going to be married.

'Come into the kitchen and I'll make you a mug of coffee while we wait for dad to bring your car back. I'm Nicole by the way, Nicole Wright and you are?'

'Charles Burroughs.' He waited to see if she recognised his name - after all he had had some minor roles in sitcoms, but she didn't.

'Hi Charles.' She put two mugs on the worktop and held up a jar of coffee. 'Instant okay and how do you take it?'

'Black please, with a tiny bit of sugar.' He looked around, if he had to design a farmhouse kitchen it would be exactly like this. From the Aga on one wall fitting snugly into the oak cupboards to the large table in the centre with a vase of wild flowers on it - it was perfect.

'Well, sit down then.' Nicole put the mugs on the table and sat opposite him. 'So, what are you doing at the Vicarage? I haven't met the new vicar yet, is she nice?'

'I don't know, I haven't seen her either.' Charles thought the Vicarage was supposed to be empty. 'We're here to perform a Murder Mystery weekend...I'm one of the actors.'

'Brill. I used to be a member of the Kingsford Players. We did a lot of comedies I seem to remember...and pantomimes.'

214

Charles had been wracking his brains to find a reason for spending the rest of the weekend with Nicole and now he had one. 'You wouldn't like to help out would you, that is if you don't have to go and milk cows or something.'

Nicole looked down at her very expensive designer dungarees, 'Oh no, I don't work on the farm, I'm just visiting Mum and Dad for a few days. I live in London.' She finished her coffee. 'So, what would I have to do at this murder weekend?'

When it was clear that young Simon was not coming back George sat head in hand on the vacated swing. He was a broken man. He looked at his watch, unless Dickie paid him straight away there was no chance of paying the deposit on time. His wife would never forgive him, his daughter would never forgive him even the family spaniel would probably never forgive him. And all because he wanted to join an exclusive golf club. He groaned aloud it wasn't as if he was any good at golf. His handicap was astronomical.

The weather, which had promised so much when he left home that morning, became as depressing as his mood. The sun once again disappeared behind a cloud, a chilly breeze sprang up and his legs felt cold. All he wanted was to get back into his own clothes and creep home. At least Alan would be well on his way to Wells with the Bishop by now so couldn't gloat when he had to tell Dickie the weekend couldn't continue.

He stood up and trudged back to the Vicarage in his broken shoes and hoped Dickie wouldn't make him pay for them.

Henrietta had not been best pleased to have to go down to the Vicarage on Flora's behalf, but decided to make the best of the situation by exercising her portly cob Jemima at the same time. She climbed onto the mounting block, heaved herself into the saddle and set off down her drive past the visitors' car park, automatically noting the number of tourists who were about to take the tour round the Manor.

Turning right into the park she set off across country, taking the long way round and jumping hedges and ditches with courage and daring - provided they weren't higher than eighteen inches or wider than a foot.

Jemima's build and temperament didn't allow for anything larger and neither did Henrietta's.

Chapter 33

In Maddie's wardrobe, Alan lost his struggle with the sneeze and the resulting explosion blew the wardrobe doors open. He shut his eyes and stood as still as possible hoping Maddie wouldn't notice him. He tried to think of an excuse as to why he was in there. An episode of the sitcom 'Faulty Towers' flashed through his mind. Could he get away with saying he was checking it for woodworm?

When nothing happened, he cautiously opened one eye and then the other and saw that Maddie was out like a light. But there was no time to feel relieved, he slipped out of her room and downstairs.

As soon as he opened the front door, he thought he was seeing things, or rather not seeing things. Not only had the Bishop disappeared but so had the Morgan. He spun round three times - it definitely couldn't be seen anywhere. He went and stood where it had been parked in the faint hope that it was still there, but invisible. Nothing. Had Herbert hotwired it? And if he had would be able to drive it to the Palace? And what was the Morgan's owner going to say?

There was no answer to any of these questions, but he felt a definite lightening in his heart. The Bishop had gone, Caroline was safe, now all he had to do was get rid of Dickie and the rest of them. He wondered briefly how he would explain the state of the bathroom to his mother, but that worry was eclipsed by a little bubble of joy which pushed its way up to his mouth causing him to smile for the first time that morning.

Just to be on the safe side he went out into the road and checked in both directions. There was no Bishop in sight, but Lady Henrietta Kingsford was trotting down the road on her cob. Surely, she wasn't coming to the Vicarage. He quickly stepped back into the drive and hid down the side of the house, crossing his fingers and muttering, 'Go past, go past.' Then he heard her say 'Whoa Jemima.' And his bubble of joy deflated quicker than an under-cooked, vanilla-souffle.

He backed further down the side and backed straight into someone heading in the opposite direction. Having built up the courage to face Dickie and tell him to go, George had been thwarted by a locked back door. He recovered from the collision first. 'What are you doing here, you should be on your way to the palace?'

'The Bishop couldn't find his keys so I had to go and look for them and when I came back, he'd gone.'

'How? You were supposed to be driving him.'

'It's fine, he's driving himself,' Alan was getting exasperated, at this moment there were more important things to worry about, 'But Lady Kingsford has just arrived.'

'What! What does she want?' Just when George thought things couldn't get any worse – they had. Her ladyship would demand to know what was going on and then report back to the Bishop and he would be summoned to the palace. He would be humiliated. His only hope was that no one would answer the door and she'd go away again.

He crept past Alan and peered round the corner just in time to see Henrietta disappear inside. He also noticed the Bishop's Rover was still parked in the drive. 'How is he driving himself to the Palace when his car's still here?'

'He took that Morgan.'

George took Alan's arm and frogged marched him to the back of the house and pointed to it, 'I don't think so.'

Alan looked in the car, he looked under all the seats and then he looked under the low-slung chassis, getting oil and dirt all over his suit. Nothing. Herbert must have driven it round the back and then gone off on foot. 'He must be walking back.'

George snorted. 'It's going to take him a heck of a long time.'

But as long as Herbert was away from the Vicarage Alan wasn't bothered about how long it took. 'I don't care. As long as he thinks he's seen Caroline that's all that matters.'

He brushed some gravel off his trousers and then realised George no longer had any hold over him. Caroline was safe. 'And as soon as Lady Kingsford has gone, I'm going to tell that Dickie Wilson he and his actors and guests have got to go because I'm having nothing more to do with this charade. And you can't make me.'

To his surprise George said, 'You're absolutely right, Alan. Don't worry, I was going to tell him that anyway, so you get off home. I expect Mother is wondering where you've got to anyway.' He knew Alan's mother was a bit of a tyrant, and thanked his lucky stars he was boss in his own home, well most of time. 'With you gone he doesn't have enough actors to take all the parts anyway so he can't carry on.'

Alan felt the weight he'd been carrying all morning lifting, but there was still a niggling doubt that George didn't really mean what he was saying. He looked at him suspiciously. 'No, it's okay I'll come in with you and we'll both tell him.'

'No, really, leave it to me Alan, I'll sort it all out.'

But Alan wasn't going to leave it. 'Lady Kingsford must have gone by now,' and he tried the back door, but it was firmly locked so he and George started hammering on it and shouting.

Freda and Angela had been looking out of their bedroom window, assessing the drop to the garden below.

'If we knot all the sheets together, we should be able to abseil down.' Freda was confident it could be done. She'd once abseiled down the side of her school to raise money for school funds although in her opinion the parents had been less than generous in their sponsorship.

Angela was equally certain they would both be killed in the attempt so was relieved when she saw George come out of the back door and stagger across the rose beds. 'We can't that Church Warden's out there.'

'As soon as he's gone, we'll do it,' and Freda resumed tying the sheets together which wasn't as easy as suggested in books.

By the time she had succeeded, George was staggering back across the rose beds and try to get in the back door. They had long since given up wondering why he was still dressed as a woman.

Now they watched him run down the side of the house only to reappear two or three minutes later with the other Church Warden. They heard the hammering and shouting, but ignored it, nothing could surprise them anymore, the whole weekend was a nightmare. Thank goodness they were barricaded in because it looked as if escaping through the window wasn't going to be possible.

Freda set about unknotting the sheets which was even more difficult than tying them up. And, although she didn't want to admit it, she was starving. A cup of coffee and a stale biscuit was all she had since leaving home. Unlike Angela, she hadn't stuffed her face at the service station near Bristol, nor had she bought cakes on their visits to the Post Office.

At some stage they were going to have to go downstairs and if not try to escape at least get something to eat, and find the cloakroom.

Chapter 34

In the attic Ronald sat on Marigold's chair while she tried to cover up his black eye with concealer followed by stage makeup. Now that Charles had disappeared, she needed Ronald to form an alliance with against Dickie. But that didn't stop her rubbing the concealer in quite hard.

Ronald didn't dare complain about the pain. He knew he wouldn't get any sympathy and he needed Marigold to hide behind. He looked at his knuckles, they weren't even red so he couldn't have hit that imposter very hard. Not like the blow Charles had given him. He was going to keep well away from Charles from now on and Dickie could like it or lump it.

As soon as Henrietta saw Herbert's Rover parked on the drive, she tied Jemima to the bell pull and hammered on the front door, which swung open under the force of her blow.

She and Dickie, who had been laying the table for lunch in the dining room, stared at each other. She saw a strange man in a French maid's outfit, he saw a portly woman in tight jodhpurs who appeared to have arrived on horseback.

He mentally ran through the list of punters who had yet to turn up. He didn't think she was one half of the honeymoon couple, Tracey and Kyle Harding, or Mrs Smythe Hickson - her husband had rung to say they would arrive after lunch. So, who the heck was she?

'Can I help you madam?'

Henrietta was also perplexed, surely that slip of a girl who had been appointed vicar couldn't afford a maid, not even a male one. But Henrietta never allowed herself to be distracted long from the business in hand. And she was well used to dealing with menials. 'I'm here to see the Bishop.'

For once Dickie was almost lost for words, why did this woman want to see Ronald? 'The Bishop?'

'Yes, his wife sent me.'

Dickie was even more confused, as far as he knew Ronald hadn't seen his wife in years. 'His wife sent you?'

'Yes, is that so hard to understand? As far as I am aware, I am speaking the Queen's English.'

Dickie thought it was very hard to understand, but he didn't dare say so. Whoever this woman was she had an air of authority about her? He gave a quick bob. 'Of course, won't you come in madam and I'll go and fetch him.'

He was about to lead the way to the drawing room, but Henrietta, who knew her way round the Vicarage better than he did, beat him to it.

'I shall wait for him in here. And I will want to see the vicar afterwards.' And with that she closed the door on him.

Dickie rushed up stairs and told Ronald who turned pale. 'A friend of my wife?' He wracked his brains trying to remember the last time he'd seen his wife and whether he owed her money? 'So, what's the name of this friend?'

Not wanting to admit he'd been too cowed to ask the women, Dickie ignored the question. 'Did you tell your wife you were coming down here?'

'Are you kidding, she'd be the last person I'd tell.'

'So, how did she know?'

'Perhaps this *friend*,' Marigold heavily italicised the word friend, 'recognised you when you were running round the village without your trousers on and rang your wife.' She'd been given a blow-by-blow account of Ronald's kidnapping and brave escape from the hound from hell and didn't believe a word of it.

Dickie said, 'She must be local I think she came on a horse.'

Ronald struggled to remember who he'd waved to on his way back to the Vicarage, but he was certain none of them were on horseback, 'No, I didn't see anyone with a horse.'

'Well, she's in the drawing room waiting for you and I don't think she's going to leave until she's seen you, so you'd better go down there and sort this out.' Dickie looked round the attic, 'Where's Charles? I told him to come and apologise.'

'He's not been up here, has he Ronald.'

'Damn! She wants to see the vicar as well, so she must mean Charles.'

'Why would a friend of your wife want to see Charles?' Marigold felt a twinge of jealousy, she was hoping to have a little dalliance with him herself.

Ronald was flummoxed, why indeed? He decided he wasn't going to face the woman on his own. 'You'll both have to come with me or I shan't go.'

They crept downstairs and listened outside the drawing room door where they could hear the ominous tapping of a riding boot on a parquet floor.

Henrietta looked at her watch, surely it couldn't take that long to find Herbert. She was about to go and look for him herself when the door opened.

'Here's the Bishop madam,' and Dickie pushed Ronald in ahead of them.

Henrietta drew herself up to her full height, did these people think she was an idiot. 'That's not the Bishop.' She peered at him closely – great heavens the man was wearing makeup.

Dickie was confused and not a little irritated, 'Well he's the only one we've got.'

'I'm talking about Herbert, man, Herbert.'

Dickie frowned, the name rang a bell, then realised she must mean the farmer Herbert Bishop. It made sense now, she looked the sort to own all the land in the village, he was probably one of her tenants. Not wanting to get the wretched man into any trouble he said, 'Oh, that Bishop. He was here earlier, but he's gone home.'

Henrietta was furious, how dare Herbert go home after she'd taken the trouble to come and see him. He must have crept out while she was waiting in the drawing room and driven off.

She glared at the three people facing her – they had colluded in this offence and she had no idea who they were. 'Who are you people and what are you doing here?'

Dickie recovered first, 'Ah yes, if it please you ma'am this is Lady Alicia and I'm her maid…oh and this is Bishop Ronald.'

Henrietta snorted, Lady Alicia was certainly no lady and Ronald looked more like ham actor than a bishop. And as for the so-called maid, well, the less said about him the better. 'And what are you all doing here?'

Dickie gave up strangling his larynx and said, 'We are holding a murder mystery weekend.'

Henrietta narrowed her eyes, 'And the vicar is happy about this?'

'I imagine so, but it's George Williams who's organising it. He's the Church Warden.'

'I know who he is, but why is he organising this, this…charade?'

'It's to raise money for the church roof fund.'

She looked at Marigold and Ronald, 'And you are all part of this?' They nodded, but didn't dare speak. Henrietta had that effect on people.

Dickie explained how the weekend worked with guests trying to detect who had committed the murder.

'And people pay to attend weekends like this?' Henrietta narrowed her eyes even more. She applauded all efforts to raise money. Heaven knows she was constantly having to raise money herself just to keep Kingsford Manor's roof from falling off. 'And how much money will this weekend raise for the roof fund?'

'Five hundred pounds.'

Henrietta did a quick calculation, Kingsford Manor had twice if not three times more bedrooms than the Vicarage. 'Would you pay me two thousand pounds to hold one of these weekends at my place?'

Dickie gulped, 'It would depend how big your place is.'

'Oh, I think you'll find Kingsford Manor's plenty big enough.'

Dickie gulped again, but he was already seeing the advertising leaflets – "Murder at the Manor", "Enjoy a weekend of crime and passion in a stately home". 'I'm sure something can be arranged...ummm, madam,' He assumed the woman must own the Manor, but was she plain missus or what?

'Right, that's settled then. I'll send my butler over to complete the arrangements this afternoon.'

'Excellent...ummm madam.' Then he had a brainwave, 'So what name shall I put on the paperwork?'

Henrietta gave him one of her glacial looks, 'Lady Kingsford of course. And what is all that banging and shouting, it sounds as if someone is trying break in? Is it part of the act?'

Dickie, hoping she hadn't noticed, quickly said it was.

'Well, I don't want anyone hammering like that on the Manor doors, some of them are more than five hundred years old.' And with that she swept out into the hall just as Freda and Angela were creeping down the stairs.

Henrietta turned to Dickie, 'And are these people guests or actors?'

227

'Oh guests. May I introduce them to your ladyship?' Henrietta inclined her head which Dickie took as a yes. 'This is Mrs Angela Mortimer and Miss Freda Andrews.' He smiled at the sisters. 'This is Lady Kingsford of Kingsford Manor.'

Henrietta again inclined her head and asked if they were enjoying their weekend. Angela looked at Freda for guidance, were they enjoying it? She thought probably not, which was why they were trying to escape.

Henrietta ignored their silence, she was used scaring members of the public speechless so carried on, 'I'm sure you are, and you must both come for the weekend when I hold one of these shindigs.' She turned back to Dickie, 'Well goodbye Mr Wilson it's been nice doing business with you.' Then she looked at Ronald and checked his muscles, he seemed quite strong, 'And you can give me a leg up.'

Dickie quickly added, 'Onto her ladyship's horse.' He didn't want Ronald thinking it was a euphemism for sex.

Freda watched them go out of the front door. As soon as she'd seen Henrietta's frayed riding jacket and patched jodhpurs, she knew she was a genuine lady. Half the parents of her school were like that – asset rich and cash poor. They would arrive to fetch their offspring in their ancient Rolls', held together with baler twine and duct tape. She glared at Marigold, not like that one, she definitely wasn't a lady.

'Oh Freda, what about that, we've been invited to a weekend at Kingsford Manor.' Angela was almost incoherent with excitement.

Dickie believed in striking while the iron was hot, 'Absolutely. So, ladies, if you'd like to book now for 'Murder at the Manor' I can give you a discount.'

'What are you talking about giving us a discount? Lady Kingsford has invited us to go as guests.' Freda was outraged.

Angela added, 'That's right.'

'Well yes, but it will be a Murder Mystery Weekend, like this, so you have to pay.' Seeing their blank looks, the light dawned on Dickie, 'Of course your daughter paid didn't she Mrs Mortimer, but surely she must have told you what this weekend was about.'

Then the light dawned on Freda, Angela's birthday present wasn't two days in a country hotel and it wasn't a retreat either – they were taking part in some theatrical enterprise. Death would be preferable to admitting she hadn't realised everything was play acting so Freda snapped, 'Of course she told us.'

She grabbed Angela's arm, 'Come along Angela we have to go to the Post Office.' She didn't want her sister saying the wrong thing - and even more important, they had to get their letter to the Archbishop back.

'But I don't want to go again.'

'Yes, you do Angela.' And she pulled her unwilling sister out of the front door.

Dickie wondered if he could risk asking them to buy something for lunch, but they were gone before he could pull out his wallet.

'So that woman was the lady of the manor,' Marigold sniffed, 'she doesn't look as if she had two pennies to rub together.'

Ronald came back in rubbing his back, 'She might be a lady but she weighs a ton and her bloody horse trod on my foot.'

But before anyone could commiserate with him, which they probably wouldn't have done anyway, the loud hammering on the back door started up again.

Telling Marigold and Ronald to mingle, Dickie headed to the kitchen. They waited until he'd gone and then headed for the dining room for a restorative gin.

Chapter 35

As Tom and Edna finally approached the Vicarage, they saw a woman on a horse come out of the drive and head towards them. Tom immediately pulled the car onto the verge, stopped the engine and got out to check there was no other traffic about. Seeing that the road was empty he waved the rider on and was given a brief nod of the head in acknowledgement.

Behind the rider, two elderly ladies also came out of the drive and were rushing down the road, one more enthusiastically than the other. He smiled at them but their conversation was so intense they didn't notice him.

He was about to get back into the driving seat when he saw a figure stagger out of a ditch, lurch across the road in front of the car and abruptly sit down on the grass.

'What the dickens…?' He looked at this watch, eleven forty-two exactly – far too early in the day be drunk and disorderly. 'Pass the breathalyser over dear I'm going to test that man.'

He walked across to Herbert and pulled him to his feet. 'Now then sir, this won't do you know, this won't do at all. How much have you been drinking?' As he was brushing some grass off Herbert's trousers, he noticed the purple shirt. 'And you a bishop too. Been at the communion wine again, have we?'

Herbert swayed slightly, but glared back, 'You might have been, but not one drop has passed my lips.'

'Well, we'll just see about that sir, we'll just see about that.' and Tom took the breathalyser from Edna who had finally found it hidden under Tom's Snoopy Dog pyjamas. He peered at Herbert's face. 'It looks as if you have been in a fight as well. I don't know what the clergy is coming to these days, I really don't.' He held out the breathalyser, 'Just blow in this tube as hard as you can please sir.'

'I most certainly will not, who the dickens are you?'

'Police sergeant Tom Cowden, now blow into the tube.'

Herbert was furious. Great heavens he was on the Chief Constable's Christmas card list and here was some jumped-up copper who wasn't even in uniform trying to breathalyse him. 'Now look here officer, I haven't been drinking, nor have I been indulging in fisticuffs. I…I was involved in a slight accident.' He tried desperately to remember what the accident was and then he found a stray thought rolling round in his head - he wanted to see his new vicar, yes that was it. 'I am trying to get to Kingsford Vicarage to see the vicar.'

'Why, that's where we're going as well.' Edna peered at him from under Tom's arm. At five foot one to his six foot three she'd spent much of her married life peering from under his arms or round his waist. In fact, some people had never seen her in her entirety.

'Now leave this to me dear.'

'But…'

But Tom was adamant; he didn't want civilians, not even his wife, interfering in his investigations. 'You say you need to get to the Vicarage to see the vicar, might I ask why sir?'

'I don't see it's any of your business, but I am trying to see the new incumbent who happens to be the first lady vicar in the diocese, probably the whole country.' Herbert puffed out his chest with pride. 'Not everyone agrees with them you know,' and a vision of his wife laying down the law earlier in the year quickly deflated him again, 'but I was determined.' He swayed slightly. 'So, if you would be so good as to take me to her.'

'All in good time sir, all in good time. Now you say you were involved in a slight accident, was that in your car?'

'No, definitely not.' Herbert laid his fingers across his lips trying to capture another memory and cogitated for several seconds then added, 'I think a picture fell on my head.'

Tom looked around. 'I can't see any picture sir.'

'No, it's not out here,' said Herbert testily. 'It was in the Vicarage.'

'So, what are you doing out here?'

'That's what I've been asking myself, one minute I was in the hall and the next thing I remember is falling in the ditch - it's all a bit of a mystery.'

Edna could contain herself no longer. 'It's all part of the plot Tom, don't you see.'

'Of course, I do dear, of course I do, but please allow me to conduct my enquiries in my own way.' He turned back to Herbert. 'I think the best plan is to get you back to the Vicarage and I will interview the female vicar and see what she has to say.'

'Good luck with that,' said Herbert, 'I've been trying to talk to her ever since I arrived.'

'So, am I right in saying you've already been to the Vicarage but you haven't seen her yet?'

'I think I have. I remember saying hello to someone and then it all went black.' Herbert clutched his head, but the only other vague memory was of Caroline swaying on an unsuitable pair of high heels. 'But it was totally unsatisfactory, I want to talk to her about the church roof fund, or lack thereof.'

Tom could hardly contain his excitement. He couldn't wait to get to the Vicarage and start interrogating suspects and the first on his list after the Bishop was this female vicar. He could see the entrance to the Vicarage a few yards down the road, but he insisted on squashing Herbert into the back of his car amongst the various bags and boxes despite Herbert's protests.

There was no way he was going to lose an important witness.

Chapter 36

As soon as Dickie unlocked the back door, he noticed George wasn't carrying any bags. 'George your hands seem strangely empty where's the food for lunch?'

George started telling him about the small boy, who'd taken the money but never came back, and sitting on the swing, and the broken shoes. He pushed the remaining twenty pounds into Dickie's hand, 'But here's the rest of your money.'

Finally, Alan could contain himself no longer. 'You have to leave Mr Wilson, now, at once.'

George snapped, 'I was just about to tell him that Alan.'

'I'm not going anywhere,' and Dickie picked up a pile of plates and headed for the dining room. His temper was not improved by finding Ronald and Marigold slurping gin. 'I told you to mingle…and where's Charles?'

Marigold shrugged, 'I've no idea, I'm not my lover's keeper.'

Dickie took the half empty gin bottle out her hand and glared at her, 'Well, do something useful Marigold and finish laying the table. And Ronald, go and wash your hands you've got mud all over them.'

'I'm not surprised that woman's boots were covered in it.'

Dickie headed back to the kitchen and met George and Alan in the hall, still arguing about who should tell him. Then they both started shouting at him. Thank goodness the two old dears weren't here to see it - they'd have barricaded themselves in again.

As he was nearest the phone when it rang Dickie answered it and wished he hadn't. Now he had a third person shouting in his ear. Before he could ask who she was, the woman on the other screamed that the caterers hadn't had their deposit paid so were threatening to cancel everything.

'What!' He held the phone out to George, 'It's some woman about the caterers, they are threatening to cancel as they haven't been paid, no wonder they haven't turned up. And you told me they were on their way.'

'But they are.'

'In which case, perhaps you could sort this out,' Dickie's voice was getting icier

George held the phone as if it was red hot and gingerly said, 'Hello.'

His wife's voice blasted his ear drum. 'Why are you still at the Vicarage when you should be in Nailsea paying the deposit. You know they have to leave at twelve thirty for another catering job…and who was that man who answered the phone?'

As soon as he heard his wife's voice, he completely forgot he had given up all hope of paying the deposit - for the second time that morning George really wished he had a mobile phone, then he could have told his wife he was in Nailsea and about to pay over the money. Now he

236

was going to have to explain why he wasn't. 'You won't believe this dear….'

'No, I won't.'

George struggled on, 'But…Caroline organised some cleaning company to come and give the Vicarage a good going over…so that's why I had to be here…until they finished.'

'Well, I hope you're satisfied, because you've ruined our daughter's wedding.'

'But I'm going straight there now to sort it out.'

'You'd better.' And the phone was slammed down.

George turned back to Dickie, 'That was my wife, she was talking about the caterers for our daughter's wedding.'

Dickie was glad he'd never married - he'd never seen a man turn so pale. 'So, she wasn't talking about our caterers?'

'Oh, good heavens no, ours are definitely on their way.'

Dickie was intrigued, 'Am I right in thinking she doesn't know about the Murder at the Vicarage.'

Before George could answer Alan leapt in, 'No one knows, not even the vicar which is why you all have to leave.'

'Don't be ridiculous old love, we can't leave now, we've only just got started.'

Alan grabbed Dickie's arm, 'But it's a disaster. You've lost three actors and the caterers haven't turned up.'

'If I let little things like that stop me, I'd have given up years ago.' And memories of Eastbourne flashed across his mind again. 'You know the old saying "It'll be alright on the night".'

Alan didn't know the old saying and anyway it was morning, but before he could reply the front door swung open and two people stood smiling at them.

Chapter 37

To say that Dickie was pleased to see the couple laden with bags and boxes of food would be an understatement. He almost offered a reduction on the cost of the weekend on the spot, but managed to contain himself. If he could get his hands on all that grub, lunch would be improved immeasurably.

'You must be Mr and Mrs Cowden, how lovely to see you, come in come in, I'm Dickie Wilson.' He reached out and took one of the boxes overflowing with quiches and packets of crisps. 'I'm afraid we don't allow food in the bedrooms, so I'll put this in the kitchen for you.' He turned to George, 'George, could you give Mrs Cowden a hand with those carrier bags and bring them through as well.'

Alan was about to tell them they had to go when he saw to his horror Herbert following them through the front door.

Dickie saw him at the same moment and said, 'What's he doing back here?'

Tom took Herbert's arm and pulled him further into the hall, 'We've just given him a lift.'

And Edna added, 'He says he's the bishop and he wants to have a chat with a vicar who's woman.'

But Dickie had had enough and thrusting the box at Alan he seized hold of Herbert's shoulder, smartly turned him round and gave him a less than gentle shove back out of the door. 'You really need to go home, I'm sure your wife is getting worried, she's probably out looking for you.'

At the mention of his wife Herbert stiffened and looked round - surely Flora wouldn't come looking for him. For one panic-stricken moment he had a vision of her hauling him back to the palace and banning all further outings apart from Cathedral services where she could keep an eye on him.

But she didn't know where he was, did she? This thought gave him no comfort - Flora, was blessed with mind-reading skills which went far beyond any television showman. Had she taken up poker she would have won a fortune. Adrenaline coursed through his stomach - this would be the first place she would come looking. She mustn't find him here. He looked round for the Rover, saw it parked by the hedge and headed for it.

Tom stared after him and then back at Dickie. 'I'd rather hoped to interview him.'

'Oh, he's not a bishop he's just a local farmer who's gone a bit doolally, he's got nothing to do with this weekend.' And Dickie quickly shut the front door.

'He certainly seemed in a very confused state.'

And Edna added, 'he said a picture fell on his head.'

'Well, if it did, it certainly wasn't here.' Dickie turned to Alan, 'Perhaps you and George could put it all this food in the kitchen.' When they didn't move, he added, 'Like now,' and waited for them to go.

Then turning back to Edna, he said, 'I'm sure you don't want any of that food to go to waste do you Mrs Cowden, so how about I put it in with our buffet lunch.'

If, a little later, Edna noticed that her food predominated at the buffet lunch she didn't say anything.

Tom couldn't care less about the food, after all he'd had cereal, a full English breakfast and two rounds of toast before leaving home; all he cared about was not missing any of the excitement. Was Mr Wilson trying to put him off the scent by claiming the Bishop was a local farmer and not a real cleric at all? 'He also claimed he'd briefly met the vicar, a woman called Caroline, according to him.'

'Well that just shows he's lost the plot, there's no female vicar here Mr Cowden.'

Tom ears pricked up at the word plot. Was this a clue? He had also registered that Mr Wilson was dressed as a maid and the man called George was dressed as a female vicar. Curious. But, like any good detective he was keeping an open mind and not jumping to conclusions.

In the kitchen a relieved George started unpacking the cakes and quiches, the crisps and the sandwiches, the hard-boiled eggs and fruit and finally two bottles of wine. His optimism returned. Surely Dickie would pay him, now there was plenty of food - all he had to do was ring the caterers and say he was on his way. He spread the largess out on the worktop. 'There's more than enough here for lunch.'

Alan glared at him, 'Blow the lunch, what are we going to do about the Bishop.'

'I told you before, drive him back to the Palace.'

'And I told you he's lost his car keys.'

'So, get a taxi. In the meantime, I've got a phone call to make.' He headed to the hall only to find Dickie introducing Ronald and Marigold to Tom and Edna.

'This is Ronald the real Bishop. Bishop this is Mr and Mrs Cowden. And this is Lady Alicia who is also staying with us. And here's George ready to take your luggage upstairs.' He signalled to George and pointed at a suitcase. 'So, let's all go into the drawing room and get to know each other.'

But Tom didn't want to mingle with the others, he was itching to set up shop. 'Is there a room where I could set up my white board and interview people?'

Dickie was taken aback, he'd been impressed with the sisters who'd got into the swing of things, but this was taking the weekend to a whole new level. 'I say old love, you're really taking this seriously.'

And Edna added, 'That's because he's a police sergeant.'

Tom should have added retired, but decided that could come later. 'I could do with some help with my equipment.'

Dickie felt his stomach lurch, why did Eastbourne keep coming to mind. He'd better keep this one sweet. 'I guess you could use the library, it's down there next to the cloakroom. George, could you give Sergeant Cowden a hand.' Then he guided Edna, Marigold and Ronald into the drawing room.

George looked out of the front door - Herbert, was still in the drive violently shaking the door handle of his Rover. He didn't think the Bishop would recognise him, but just in case he kept his back to him as much as possible as he helped Tom unload his car and carry a large box of equipment and a white board into the library.

When he came back into the hall it was empty so he took the chance to ring the wedding caterers and plead for more time, but before he could finish dialling Tom came back in the front door balancing the Polaroid camera and tape recorder under one arm and guiding Herbert along with the other. George put the phone down and eased back towards the kitchen, hoping Herbert hadn't seen him.

Tom took hold of Herbert's arm, 'If you'd just like to step this way please sir, it won't take long.'

Herbert peered at the man, he wished he could find his glasses then the world wouldn't be so blurred, 'Who are you?'

'I've already told you sir I'm Police sergeant Cowden and I shall be asking you a few questions in a minute.'

Herbert racked his brains, had he done anything wrong? Had Flora sent the man to arrest him for stealing his own car? That thought made him go weak at the knees again.

'What questions? I didn't steal the Rover it's mine.'

'All in good time sir, all in good time. But first I'm going to start by taking your photograph to pin on my white board and then I'm going to finger print you.'

George waited until they were safely in the library and then went into the kitchen to tell Alan - but Alan was nowhere to be seen.

Chapter 38

Alan had dithered in the kitchen. It was all very well for George to say ring for a taxi, but unless he could use the Vicarage phone, he would have to run to the Post Office and use the public call box. And there was no guarantee the Bishop would stay put until the taxi arrived. Finally, he crept out of the backdoor and looked round the drive, the Rover was still there, but once again Herbert had disappeared. But there was no bubble of happiness this time because he knew that like a bad penny Herbert would turn up again unless got rid of for good.

He was standing wondering what to do when there was a screech of tires, and a spray of gravel stung the back of his neck. He swung round and saw what appeared to be another of Dickie's guests. Well, this one wasn't even going to get inside the Vicarage.

Jack Albright had arrived with a flourish, and a beaming smile. 'All right mate?'

No, he wasn't all right. The man climbing out the Mercedes epitomised everything Alan disliked, from the heavy gold jewellery to his familiar way of speaking. 'Go away,' he shouted, 'you've come to the wrong place.'

But Jack wasn't really listening. He flipped open the boot, pulled out a holdall and smoothed down his hair. 'Dickie Wilson? Jack Albright at your service, sah,' and he gave a mock salute.

'No, I'm not Dickie Wilson. There's no one here, the place is empty.'

At that moment the front door opened revealing Dickie, closely followed by George.

'Don't look empty to me mate.' But Jack *was* taken aback and wondered if he had indeed come to the wrong place. He was looking forward to two days of murder and mystery instead of which he'd stumbled on a drag weekend.

Dickie quite forgetting he was the maid, called out, 'Mr Albright? Come in old love, come in, glad you made it. George, take Mr Albright's holdall.'

Jack, somewhat reluctantly handed it over and followed Dickie inside.

As soon as they had disappeared George saw Alan heading down the drive and ran after him. 'Where are you going?'

'Home. The Bishop has disappeared again and I've had enough.'

George grabbed him, 'No, you can't.'

'Watch me,' and he pulled himself free and kept walking.'

'The Bishop is back in the Vicarage.'

Alan paused momentarily and then decided he didn't care. He'd tried his best and none of it was his fault.

George was desperate, the arrival of Edna's food had revived his hopes of getting paid. But he still needed Alan to stay long enough and act as the vicar until the money was actually in his hand.

He ran down the drive after him, 'Look, for the sake of Caroline, I'm prepared to have one more shot at pretending to be her. I'll just get rid of this holdall and as soon as the Bishop comes out of the library, I will do it.' He looked down at his skirt and torn tights, and broken shoes, 'See, I'm still dressed as her I just have to find the wig. There's just one condition.'

Alan glared at him, 'What condition?'

In the library Herbert was suffering the indignity of having his fingerprints taken. His polaroid picture, showing him staring wild-eyed at the camera, had already been stuck up on a white board with his name underneath it.

Tom gave him a tissue to wipe the ink off his digits, then put a new cassette in his tape recorder and sat down opposite him. 'I am Police Sergeant Cowden and I am interviewing...', he realised he didn't have Herbert's name and address so he turned off the recording and opened his notebook, 'Right sir, let's start with your full name and address.'

Herbert glared at him, 'I've told you all this before, I am Herbert, Bishop of Bath and Wells.'

'I just need it again for my records, sir.' Tom carefully wrote down Herbert Bishop. 'So where do you live? Is it Bath or Wells, it can't be both?'

'Wells of course.'

'And the rest of your address please.'

'The Palace, I can't remember the post code.'

'So not on a farm then.'

'On a farm! Are you mad! I'm the Bishop.'

Tom looked at Herbert noting the two black eyes, the wild hair, the mud-covered trousers and grass-stained jacket. He might be wearing a purple shirt but no way was he a bishop. 'It's probably best not to call a police officer mad, sir. And impersonating a man of the cloth is an indictable offence.' He wasn't sure about that, but he assumed Herbert wouldn't know either.

He turned the recorder back on and said, 'The witness is Herbert Bishop from Wells. Now, speak into the tape recorder, sir and tell me about this Rover. You said it was yours and you hadn't stolen it, is that correct?'

'Yes, I told you that outside.'

'Why did you think you *had* stolen it?'

'I didn't think I'd stolen it, my wife did.'

'Your wife stole it?'

'No, of course she didn't.'

'So, whose car is it, sir?'

'It's mine, look I've got the keys.' Herbert patted his pockets - nothing. 'I seem to have temporarily mislaid them.'

Tom tapped his pen thoughtfully on his lips and like all good interrogators decided to switch questions in the hope of catching Mr Bishop off guard. 'Now, tell me exactly what you are doing here?'

'I told you earlier, I'm here to see the vicar, Caroline Timberlake.'

'Oh yes, so you did sir, so you did. In fact, I seem to recall you said you already had seen her, is that correct or isn't it?'

Herbert struggled to remember, had he actually seen her or was she a figment of his imagination like his car keys? Now he was under interrogation he couldn't be sure.

Tom carried on remorselessly, 'I have made enquiries, sir and there is no female vicar on the premises,' he decided not to mention the man dressed as a female vicar at this juncture, he'd keep that up his sleeve for later, 'so what have you got to say to that?'

Herbert didn't have anything to say to that, but the policeman obviously expected an answer. 'I can't swear I saw her, but I fully intend to.'

In the drawing room Ronald, Marigold and Edna sat and stared at each other. Dickie had left when he heard the squeal of car tires and Edna had no idea how to start a conversation with a bishop and a Lady. She didn't think either of them would be interested in swapping quiche recipes or knitting patterns.

They were all relieved when Dickie came back in with another guest. 'This is Mr Jack Albright everyone. He's an artist.'

Marigold leapt up and fluttered her eyelashes at him. 'I'm Lady Alicia, I've always wanted my portrait painted.'

Ronald, hoping the newcomer would help protect him from Charles, shook Jack's hand warmly, 'And I'm Bishop Ronald old chap, good to meet you.'

Jack looked round the room and did a quick assessment of the paintings, all poor reproductions with cheap frames, the owner might be in the market for something better. 'Call me Jack everyone. So, who does this gaff belong?'

Chapter 39

Freda and Angela were now treated like old friends by the villagers who, believing they were rich because of buying a first-class stamp, all wanted to shake their hands for luck.

When they had freed themselves, Freda marched up to the counter and coughed to attract the attention of the Post Mistress who was busy making more sandwiches for lunch. When the final piece of ham had been laid between two slices of bread and garnished with chopped tomatoes and some crisps, she turned to look at her customers.

Freda stopped drumming her fingers and said, 'You probably remember us we came in earlier and bought some writing paper.'

'That's right m'dears, and then you comes back for brown paper and sticky tape, didn't you?'

'Yes quite…but on a previous visit we gave you a letter to go in the post.'

'That's right, it was addressed to the Archbishop. I remembers that because you bought a first-class stamp.' She lifted up the counter and stepped round them. 'Scuse me a minute I must just take this out to Mrs Thomas, her's getting a bit hungry.'

Freda started drumming her fingers again while she waited for the Post Mistress to come in and get settled behind her counter. 'It's about that letter...I want it back.'

The Post Mistress stared at her. 'Oh, I can't do that m'dear, I'm not allowed to touch letters once they've been posted. They belongs to the Royal Mail.'

'But technically it hasn't been posted, you dropped it into that sack behind you.'

The Post Mistress turned and looked at the sack as if surprised to see it there. 'That's right, you'm very observant.'

'So, if you could just put your hand in and take it out, I would be very grateful.'

'That's as maybe, but that letter now belongs to Her Majesty.'

'No, it doesn't it belongs to me.'

'Not once you've posted it, it don't.'

Freda could feel her temper rising, but she couldn't risk alienating the Post Mistress so she shouted at Angela instead, 'What are you looking at over there come and help me explain how important it is we get our letter back.'

Angela pulled herself away from the boxes of gobstoppers and sherbet dabs and said, 'We got it all wrong about the weekend, no one is going to get murdered or have sex so the Archbishop doesn't need to know.'

Freda glared at her - Angela's explanation wasn't helping. She turned back to the Post Mistress, who was thinking the Archbishop might not need to know, but she was certainly interested, and she'd thought of a way of finding out.

'Look m'dears I'd like to help you but me hands are tied. So, what I suggests is this - you need to write a letter to the Archbishop explaining everything in detail and telling him to ignore your first one. But you'll have to do it straight away because the mail van will be here any minute, and that's the last collection until Monday.'

Freda knew she was beaten, there was no time to go back to the Vicarage, a fact that Angela helpfully pointed out, the letter would have to be written here and now. 'I'll need another pad of writing paper and envelopes.'

'I'm sorry m'dear, but you bought the last set.' But the Post Mistress was ready with a solution. She pointed to a stand near the door which had several post cards on it showing village scenes and with the words 'Wish you were Here' printed across the front of them. 'You just got time to write one of those,' and to be helpful she gave Freda her ball point pen, and a first-class stamp on the house.

Freda quickly scribbled an explanation, handed the post card over and waited for it to be dropped into the sack. When the Post Mistress held on to it, she asked why.

'Oh, postcards are treated separately m'dear. Sometimes they gets stuck at the bottom of the sack so I hands them to the mailman personally.'

Freda viewed this explanation with suspicion, but there wasn't much she could do about it. 'Come along Angela, we'd better be getting back.'

Chapter 40

As Charles and Nicole strolled back to the Vicarage he casually said, 'As the dastardly Sir Giles I do have to kiss you…quite a lot actually,' which wasn't strictly true.

'That's okay, as the maid I'm sure I would be perfectly happy about that.'

Charles certainly felt perfectly happy. After a second leisurely coffee, Nicole had changed into an outfit more suitable for a maid and looked even more stunning. 'By the way, I never asked what you did in London.'

'I'm a model.'

Charles shot from happy to ecstatic, 'Oh my word, Marigold is going to hate you.' And he was right.

As they walked up the drive, they saw George and Alan having a heated argument.

'Look, it's Alan and Mr Williams.' Nicole waved her hand. 'Hello you two.'

Alan felt his stomach lurch, Nicole had been his first crush, but he'd never had the courage to ask her out. What was she doing here, with that actor bloke?

George's stomach also lurched, but that was because he didn't want anyone he knew, to see him dressed in a skirt. He couldn't risk a story like that going round the village - not realising that ship had already sailed. 'Nicole! How unexpected. You must be wondering what I'm doing here dressed like this.'

'No, not at all Mr Williams. Charles had been telling me about the weekend, so I've come to help out as well.'

Charles nodded in agreement, 'She's going to take the part of Marigold's maid.'

'And you're in it too aren't you Alan?' Nicole gave him a devasting smile, 'Do you remember when we were in that pantomime together? You were very good.'

A tongue-tied Alan did remember, only too well and for a moment Caroline was pushed out of his thoughts, but not for long. And seeing Nicole standing there in her short black skirt, black tights and white blouse a thought struck him.

The same thought also struck George, but would Nicole do it? 'Yes, we are both helping out aren't we Alan?'

'So what parts are you playing?'

'I'm the butler, and Alan's the vicar.'

Nicole looked at George's skirt and raised an eyebrow.

'Ah yes, well there have been several changes to the script.' George nodded to Charles, 'he was originally going to be a female vicar, then I was, oh and then Alan was...no it was the other way around then it was me.' George had long since given up trying to remember the sequence of events.

And Nicole had long since stopped listening after hearing Charles was going to play a woman, she turned to him with a big grin, 'You never mentioned that Charles.'

'It wasn't my idea, believe me. Anyway, let's go and introduce you to Dickie.'

As they walked into the drawing room all eyes were drawn to the statuesque Nicole, well, all except Ronald's, he was trying to make himself invisible, hoping Charles wouldn't notice him.

'Ah, Sir Giles, I was wondering where you'd got to.' Dickie turned to Edna and Jack, 'let me introduce Sir Giles Forsythe and…friend.'

Charles wasn't quite sure how to address Dickie who was still dressed as the maid, but talking in his normal voice. 'Could we have a word with you…outside perhaps.'

'Of course, Sir Giles, will you excuse me everyone.'

Once they were in the hall Charles introduced Nicole and Dickie grasped her hand in relief. 'You have no idea how pleased I am to see you.' He now had a full cast except George and Alan seemed to be missing. 'Have you seen those two church wardens?'

'Yes, they're outside in the drive.'

'What are they doing out there, I want them to come and mingle. Sort it out Charles while I get changed.'

Outside, George and Alan were arguing about how they could get Nicole to pretend to be Caroline. Both claimed it was their idea, but neither could say how it was going to be achieved.

Charles appeared at the front door and said, 'Dickie wants you both to come in and mingle.'

Alan's immediate reaction was to say no, but George said, 'We will in a minute, but could we have a word with Nicole first…out here.'

Charles went and got her and Nicole appeared in the doorway looking puzzled.

After a lot of false starts and disagreements Alan and George managed to tell her what they wanted her to do, stressing they were doing it for Caroline.

Nicole burst out laughing and said of course she would to it. The weekend was turning out to be much more fun than her usual visits to the family farm, and she was looking forward to spending time with Charles. 'But it will have to be quick as I have to go and look at my script.' She turned and gave Charles a quick smile, 'I can't tell you how much I'm looking forward to doing a bit of acting this weekend.'

George could suddenly see a way of keeping Alan tied to the Vicarage. 'Ah, well, I'm afraid once the Bishop has gone back to the palace Alan has to get off home so the weekend can't carry on. Dickie said it wouldn't work without Alan being the vicar so, well, everyone will have to leave.' He shrugged his shoulders as if to say he'd done his best, but it was out of his hands. 'Sorry to disappoint you.'

As he hoped, Nicole didn't do disappointment. 'Alan, surely you can stay and help out, can't you?' There was no way she was letting Charles go home before they'd really got to know each other. When Alan didn't reply she added, 'Well in that case you can get someone else to be Caroline,' and she went back indoors.

And Charles added, 'Thanks a bunch,' and disappeared as well.

George and Alan resumed their argument, but this time George refused to pretend to be Caroline, pointing out that Nicole would be much better at it than him and it was just Alan's obstinacy that was preventing a happy outcome.

Alan reiterated his argument that none of this would have happened if George hadn't hired out the Vicarage in the first place.

They were so engrossed that Freda and Angela, returning from the Post Office, were almost upon them before they noticed the sisters.

Freda raised an eyebrow at George's skirt, but said nothing except that she and Angela had had a lovely walk and were now looking forward to lunch. As soon as they had gone inside George once again tried to get Alan to change his mind and stay. Tempers flared and voices were raised.

Chapter 41

Maddie came to with a start and looked round the unfamiliar room. She had been dreaming about people shouting at each other. For a moment she had no idea where she was. Then the drinking session with Sir Giles came back to her and she decided to keep off the gin – at least until after dinner.

She stood up and noticed the wardrobe doors were wide open and her dresses were all pushed up to one end of the rail. The fact that she couldn't remember doing that was a bit worrying. She straightened them out and headed for the bathroom. For once it was unoccupied, but there was a pair of trousers soaking in the wash basin.

When she came out, she was pleased to see Charles heading along the landing. 'Sir Giles, we have to stop meeting like this.' Then she noticed Nicole and was less pleased.

Charles pulled Nicole forward, 'This is Lydia, Lady Alicia's maid.'

Maddie was surprised as she remembered seeing someone else dressed as a maid, but decided it was all part of the mystery. 'So, you're staying here as well are you Lydia?'

Nicole gave a small curtsey, 'Yes mum,' but that wasn't strictly true as Nicole said she would sleep at the farm and come in early on Sunday, despite Charles trying to persuade her that wouldn't work.

Charles said, 'I'm just showing her round the Vicarage, so if you'll excuse us,' and they headed up to the attic.

Maddie looked at her watch and, completely forgetting she wasn't going to have any more gin, went downstairs for a pre-lunch drink. She arrived in the hall at the same time as Freda and Angela came in the front door.

In the attic Dickie was caught in his boxer shorts, looking for his trousers when Nicole and Charles came in. He looked at what Charles was wearing, 'Are they mine?'

'Yes.'

'Where are yours?'

'Marigold put them in soak in the bathroom, they were a bit dirty.' He didn't like to say in front of Nicole that they were covered in mud and cow dung, she might think he was criticising her father.

'Well, I need them back.'

'Look, there's a spare pair in the cloakroom, you can have those, unless Ronald's got them now.'

'Why would he want them?'

'Because those are his in the corner, soaking wet.'

'This is ridiculous, Charles, you go and get the trousers from the cloakroom and give me back mine.'

'I don't think they'll fit me as well as yours do.'

Nicole listened to them banging on about trouser swapping, who was wearing whose and what could be done about it and decided to take charge. 'I'll go and get the trousers from the cloakroom and you two can sort them out between you. And while I'm doing that, you can put all the wet clothes in a bag and I'll pop them home to Mum and ask her to wash and tumble dry them. It won't take long and I'll bring back a couple of pairs of Dad's to be going on with.' She saw the look on Charles' face and added, 'Not his work ones, he's got some nice suits hanging in the wardrobe which he never wears.'

Dickie looked at her in admiration and Charles looked at her with adoration.

Chapter 42

After promising Maddie they would join her in the drawing room, Angela and Freda went upstairs to tidy their hair and discuss their tactics. Both had agreed to say, if asked, that they had always known it was a murder mystery weekend and were just getting into the spirit of things.

'I have a vague idea of what will happen,' Freda said, 'one of my staff went to something similar at a birthday party and at the end they had to work out who the murderer was from the clues given to them. So, we must take note of everything that happens.'

'But not to send to the Archbishop this time,' Angela ventured a small joke and hoped Freda would see the funny side – she didn't always.

Freda managed a small smile. 'Come on, we don't want to miss anything.'

In the drawing room Maddie homed in on the Jack, who had been cornered by Marigold. She held out her hand, 'We haven't met, have we, I'm Maddie Talbot.'

Jack managed to wriggle round Marigold's ample frame. 'Jack Albright – artist in residence.'

'Really, I didn't know there was one.'

'Only joking love, although I am an artist.'

'How exciting, I've never met a real live one before. I do have a lot of pictures at home though.'

Jack was immediately interested. 'I bet you've got room for one more, what sort to you like.'

It turned out Maddie's art collection was a few prints by Arthur John Elsey whose paintings of dogs, cats and ponies had enlivened many a box of chocolate or jigsaw puzzles, definitely not the kind of thing Jack would bother to copy.

But Maddie was more interested in the awkward way Jack was holding his head. 'Have you hurt your neck? Because I'm very good at giving massages.' And before he could say he was fine she'd pushed him down into a chair and was pressing her thumbs into the muscles at the top of his spine.

Marigold stared at them venomously.

Edna had perked up when Maddie entered, but soon saw she wouldn't want to talk about quiches and knitting patterns, so she sank back into the cushions and wished Tom would hurry up and come in. She knew it was his weekend, but even so he ought to keep her company.

Tom meanwhile had finished a highly satisfactory interview with Herbert Bishop and was escorting him to the front door, intent on taking him back to the Rover where he found him, so as not to upset the flow of the weekend.

Outside he saw the two men who had carried in Edna's food in a lively conversation. Both stopped as soon as they saw him and rushed over.

George reacted first, 'Where are you taking him?'

'Back to his car.' Tom then added in a whisper, 'I don't think it's really his, in fact he seems a bit bewildered so probably shouldn't be driving anyway.'

'Don't worry Mr Cowden, we'll look after him, you go and join the others.'

Tom couldn't resist saying, 'It's Sergeant Cowden,' but was more than happy to leave them all to it as he was desperate to get back to the library and play back the tape.

Alan, George and Herbert looked at each other, each wondering what to do next.

Herbert was the first to speak. Seeing George in a skirt reminded him why he was in Kingsford. 'I'm here to see the vicar, Caroline Timberlake and I'm not going anywhere until I do.'

George said, 'But you've already seen her sir, don't you remember?'

But Herbert was not being fobbed off anymore. 'No, I haven't, so please be so good as to go and fetch her and bring her out here.' He didn't want to go back inside the Vicarage in case that policeman changed his mind and decided to arrest him so he crossed his arms defiantly and stood glaring at them.

'Of course, sir, just give us a moment.'

Alan couldn't believe they were back at square one, but he didn't have time to dwell on it as George pulled him out of the Bishop's hearing. 'You heard what he said so go and tell Nicole you've changed your mind and you'll play the part of the vicar this weekend if she'll pretend to be Caroline.'

'And what are you going to do?'

'I'll take him round the back into the garden and she can talk to him there.'

And as good as his word, George led Herbert down the side of the house and could be heard saying, 'Come and sit in the sun My Lord and Mr Palmer will bring her out.'

Chapter 43

As soon as Angela and Freda came into the drawing room, Edna recognised a kindred spirit and ignoring Freda she stood up, took Angela's hand in both of hers and said, 'I'm Edna, come and sit over here with me.'

Freda looked round and nodded her head at Marigold and Ronald, 'Lady Alicia, Bishop.' Then she noticed Jack having his neck massaged by Maddie and said, 'And you are?'

'Jack Albright, artist and portrait painter. Fancy having yours done love?'

Freda bridled, no one called her love and got away with it, then she remembered she was 'going with the flow' and forced a smile, 'Not at the moment, thank you.'

She was saved from further conversation by Dickie bouncing into the room. He was feeling a lot happier now that he was back in his trousers - Charles had finally agreed to hand them over and was waiting and see what Nicole brought back from the farm before attempting to try on the pair from the cloakroom. 'Right,' he said rubbing his hands together, 'have we all met each other now.'

There were subdued murmurs of agreement so Dickie decided the atmosphere needed livening up. 'So, who'd like a glass of wine and some nibbles first before lunch?'

The murmur of agreement was much more enthusiastic.

Dickie headed to the kitchen, once again giving thanks to which ever deity looked after impresarios, for the gift of Edna's food and wine. He was even more delighted when he saw Alan coming in the front door, his cast was nearly complete. 'Ah, there you are old love. Hang on a minute you need this,' and he pulled a dog collar out of his pocket, 'put it on and go in the drawing room and mingle.'

Mingling was the last thing Alan had in mind at that moment. He was caught between a rock and a hard place and he was not happy about it. To save Caroline from disaster he was being forced to spend the weekend pretending to be a vicar with a load of strangers most of whom terrified him.

'And where's George? I need him here to help me serve some wine and nibbles.'

'I'll tell him as soon as I see him. Umm do you know where Nicole is?'

'In the attic, she'll be down in a minute, so while you're waiting go and meet everyone.'

Alan waited until Dickie had gone into the kitchen then headed up the stairs as fast as he could. He knocked timidly on the door which was opened by Nicole carrying a plastic bag full of what looked like wet clothes.

'Oh, Alan, what do you want?' She sounded frosty.

'I…I've changed my mind, I'll take part this weekend, but please, you've got to come and pretend you're Caroline.'

Nicole beamed at him. 'I'll do it as soon as I've taken this washing home.' And gave him a quick hug and a kiss on the cheek.

Alan blushed, but he was determined to continue, 'No, there's no time, you have to see the Bishop now, he's in the garden...please Nicole.'

She kept him waiting a moment for a reply and then laughed and said of course she'd go do it. Alan gave her his dog collar which she fitted under her blouse collar. Then he looked at her hair, 'You need the blonde wig.'

'Okay, where is it?'

Alan had no idea.

Chapter 44

The minute Herbert saw the Morgan, he climbed back into it. George debated whether to ask him to get out, but decided that at least it was keeping him distracted while they waited for Nicole. Fortunately, Herbert wasn't interested in talking so George's only worry was Dickie looking out of the window and throwing the Bishop out of his car.

After wrenching the wheel round a few times Herbert announced the steering was slack and asked George where the nearest garage was.

'In Clevedon, My Lord, but we don't have time to take it there.' He looked at his watch, how much longer was Alan going to be. Then he heard a 'pssst' and saw Alan peering round the side of the house, waving at him.

Judging it was safe to leave the Bishop, he whispered 'Will she do it?'

'Yes, she's here, but we can't find the wig. Oh, and Dickie's looking for you, he needs help with the food.'

George walked round the corner and saw Nicole, who ran her fingers down her plait, smiled and said, 'Sorry, wrong colour hair.'

He thought back to when he was last wearing it. It seemed like days ago. He had it on in the hall when the Bishop got thumped for the second time. He flicked through in his memory - where did he go after that?

Finally, it came to him. 'It's under a bush in the garden. I'll go and get it.'

Thankfully Herbert was still engrossed with the Morgan so George was able to pull the wig out without him seeing it. It was full of leaves plus a small slug and a couple of earwigs, but George gave it a good shake and took it back to Nicole. She looked at it in disgust, but ran her fingers through it to get out most of the tangles and put it on.

'Alan, you take her round and introduce her, I'm going to get changed and find Dickie.'

Now that they had someone who really looked like Caroline, Alan felt a lot happier so while George disappeared round the front he and Nicole headed for the Bishop.

'Excuse me sir, but you wanted to see the vicar, well here she is.'

If Nicole was surprised to see Herbert sitting in a Morgan, she took it in her stride. 'Good morning, sir, I'm so sorry to have kept you waiting.'

Herbert squinted up at her, she looked taller than he remembered. If only he had his glasses. He glared at Alan, 'Have you seen my glasses anywhere?'

'I think you may have trodden on them, sir.'

'Rubbish, I never tread on my glasses.'

'I think they fell off and you didn't notice them.' Alan didn't elaborate on why they had fallen off.

Herbert grunted and turned to Nicole. 'So, my dear how are you settling in?'

'Very well sir, the vicarage is lovely and the congregation has been very welcoming.'

'Good, good. That's what I like to hear. Now about the…'

But Nicole hadn't finished yet, 'and as for the Church Wardens they have been wonderful,' and realising Herbert couldn't see her clearly, she winked at Alan, who blushed again.

'Quite right, and so they should be. Now about the church roof fund - do you have any ideas on how to raise some money because the diocese can't pay for the repairs?'

Nicole hesitated for a fraction of a second then said, 'I was thinking of holding a Murder Mystery weekend in the Vicarage. I've heard of other parishes doing it and they have been very successful.'

Alan waited for the Bishop to explode, but instead he said, 'That's excellent, much better than endless jumble sales and cake stalls.'

'Yes, that's what I thought, I'm so glad you like the idea.'

'I knew I'd picked the right person when I asked you to take on the living Caroline, well done my dear, you are a breath of fresh air.'

'Thank you, sir.'

Alan couldn't believe it was going so smoothly, but he still needed to keep the Bishop out of the Vicarage. 'Would you like me to call you a taxi, sir?'

'No need I have my car and he patted the steering wheel.'

'But without your glasses, sir don't you think it would be better to leave it here and I'll arrange for someone to return it to the palace.'

Herbert was loth to relinquish the Morgan, but conceded he might be safer in a taxi.

Alan whispered to Nicole he'd pop home and phone for one, but Nicole thought he might be tempted to stay at home once he'd done that so whispered back, 'No, it's okay I'll get my brother to take him, he won't mind and it will be a lot quicker.' She smiled at Herbert, 'I have to go and write my sermon now sir, but it's been lovely meeting you again.'

Alan watched her disappear round the corner and wondered how to entertain the Bishop until her brother arrived. But the sun was back out and it was pleasantly warm in the south-facing garden so Herbert seemed more than happy sitting in the Morgan. Alan thought all he needed was a large pair of yellow driving gloves and he would look exactly like Toad of Toad Hall.

Chapter 45

After leaving Alan to deal with the Bishop, George headed for the cloakroom. Most of his clothes were still on the floor apart from his trousers. He crept into the kitchen hoping he may have left them in there.

'Have you seen my trousers Dickie?'

'No, where did you leave them?'

'In the cloakroom.'

'Ah, Charles has got them.'

'What! Why?'

'He was wearing mine so Nicole went and got yours for him.'

George felt he'd walked into a Whitehall farce. 'So, what am I supposed to wear?'

'It's okay old love, she's bringing back some spare pairs, she won't be long.' He pushed a tray of drinks into George's hands, 'Take these into the drawing room and hand them round.'

'But I want my trousers not someone else's.'

'You can sort that when she comes back.'

George gave up on the trousers, but he wasn't prepared to give up on the money. 'About the five-hundred pounds.'

'Ah yes old love, I've been thinking about that, and now you're part of the cast I'll pay you at the same time as I pay the others - it's only fair.' Dickie had no intention of letting George slip off early.

'When will that be?'

'Sunday afternoon.'

In the drawing room the conversation was much more animated. As Edna had hoped, Angela was more than happy to sit and talk about quiche recipes and knitting patterns with her. And, much to Freda's relief, Lady Alicia and Maddie were both competing for the attentions of that common artist, Jack or whatever his name was.

Deciding the only person of merit in the room was the Bishop, she strode across to Ronald. The last time she'd seen him he was lying apparently unconscious in the hall. Unsure if that was all part of the weekend, she decided not to mention it. 'So, My Lord, this is all good fun isn't it?' Freda was determined to show she was enjoying herself, but it didn't look as if the bishop was if his twitching face was anything to go by.

Ronald was keeping a wary eye on the door to the hall. He'd heard Charles' voice earlier and was dreading him coming into the room. When the door handle moved, he hid behind Freda, but it was George bearing a tray of drinks followed by Dickie with bowls of crisps and tiny toasted cheese sandwiches he'd quickly cooked under the grill.

In the library, Tom was getting himself better organised. He moved the writing desk so that it faced the door and set up his finger-printing kit on the window sill along with the breathalyser. He listened to Mr Bishop's tape one more time and then stopped the recording so that it was ready for the next suspect. All he needed now was another interviewee.

In the hall he saw Mr Wilson, who was now wearing trousers and carrying a tray into one of the rooms followed by the butler, who still wasn't, and made a mental note of it.

Entering behind them, he was introduced round the room as Sergeant Cowden, and he couldn't help noticing that the man having his neck massaged, had turned pale. He had his next interviewee. 'I wonder if Mr Albright would be happy to come and have a chat in the library.'

Jack thought no he wouldn't, but that might make him look suspicious. He'd come to Kingsford as much to get away from the Old Bill as dodgy art collectors. All he wanted was a relaxing weekend, perhaps with a spot of business thrown in. He knew he was taking part in a murder mystery, but that copper looked legit.

But Maddie wasn't prepared to lose him yet so told Tom to find someone else as Jack's neck still needed a lot more massaging.

As far was Jack was concerned, she could massage his neck as long as she wanted. It was very relaxing and he'd quite forgiven her for her choice of art.

Chapter 46

Nicole ran back to the farm and gave the washing to her mother with a quick explanation as to why it needed to be done asap. Then she shot up stairs to her parents' bedroom and flipped through the wardrobe until she found a couple of pairs of suitable trousers. Then she dashed outside and found her brother tinkering with his souped-up Honda.

Within ten minutes she was back at the Vicarage with trousers, car and brother Henry. Between her, Alan and Henry they managed to prise Herbert out of the Morgan into the Honda. Alan's heart was in his mouth as the car roared out of the drive and, leaving a smell of burning rubber behind, disappeared down the road. But his concern was more than offset by the relief that the Bishop had finally gone.

He'd done it, he'd really done it. Caroline was saved. He followed Nicole in the front door and put the dog collar round his neck - it felt like a chain, and he still had to go home at some time and face his mother, but for the moment he felt a tiny bit happy.

Dickie was heading back to the kitchen for the other bottle of wine when Nicole came in the front door.

'Can you tell Mr Williams I've got some trousers for him.' Then she headed up the stairs. He watched her for a moment as she took them two at a time and ruefully thought how great it was to be young and energetic then turned to Alan. 'I'll introduce you to everyone as the vicar, just wait here a second.'

In the attic Charles looked at the two pairs Nicole had brought him and then at George's - none of them looked a good fit, but by rolling George's over at the waist and keeping his jacket done up he hoped they would do.

After a quick kiss, for practice, they made their way to the drawing room, where Dickie was topping up the wine glasses. As soon as he saw them, he said, 'For those who haven't met them yet this is Sir Giles Forsythe and Lydia, Lady Alicia's maid.'

Freda noted Lady Alicia looked more surprised than anyone when she saw her maid. Freda was a bit confused herself as last time the maid was Mr Wilson dressed as a woman. But, determined to 'keep going with the flow' she kept her thoughts to herself.

To say that Marigold was surprised to see the new Lydia was an understatement - she was furious. And it didn't take her long to twig that there was something going on between this woman and Charles. As soon as Dickie offered her some crisps she hissed, 'Who the hell is she?'

Dickie hissed back, 'Someone who is helping us out so don't make a fuss.'

Marigold wasn't the only one in a fury, George was seething as well. As soon as Dickie introduced Alan to everyone as the vicar, he was treated like one of the guests. As George handed him a glass of wine he hissed, 'You're enjoying this aren't you?'

Alan glared at him - he definitely wasn't. He was terrified that Maddie knew he'd been in her wardrobe and would start asking awkward questions or, even worse, she'd start trying to give him first aid again.

Meanwhile Ronald was trying to hide himself in the corner hoping Charles wouldn't notice him. It didn't work and Charles walked across and said, 'Can I see you outside a moment Bishop?'

Ronald looked round the room wild-eyed, 'No you can't,' and pushed further back against the wall.

Charles leaned in closer and whispered, 'There's a pair of trousers for you in the attic.'

Convinced that Charles was trying to lure him upstairs to thump him again he whispered, 'No go away, I'm talking to this dear lady,' and tried to hide behind Freda again.

Charles shook his head in exasperation and got even closer, 'I'm trying to help you, up in the attic there's some trousers for you.'

'Really, you're not trying to trick me.'

'No, Nicole brought them round, and yours are being washed and dried.'

Ronald had no idea who Nicole was and didn't really care. A nasty draught had been blowing up his cope and he couldn't sit down without showing his legs to the ladies. He was so overcome with emotion he nearly hugged Charles.

When Dickie whispered to George that his trousers were in the attic, George didn't need telling twice. In fact, he and Ronald were so desperate that they both tried to get through the door at the same time.

Henry's car fairly flew across the Mendips, much quicker, Herbert thought, than taxis normally travelled, which meant he was back at the palace sooner than he wanted.

If he'd hoped to creep in unnoticed, he was wrong. Arms crossed fiercely across her chest Flora took in his two black eyes, his bruised and battered frame covered in mud and grass stains and concluded he'd smashed the Rover as well as his glasses

'Please don't expect any sympathy, Herbert. I don't know how you managed to start your car, but now you have crashed it let that be a lesson to you, because you are not going to have new one.' She tried to think of an apposite biblical quotation - but couldn't. Instead, she held out the tennis ball and wire strippers. 'I found these in the garage, I don't know what you used them for, but I am confiscating them.'

Herbert watched her storm off to the kitchen. If confiscating his hot-wiring kit was all the punishment he was going to get, then he'd got off lightly. His memories of the morning were a bit hazy in places, but he'd seen Caroline and she was going to raise money for the church roof fund - which at the end of the day was all that mattered.

Ronald got to the attic first and was trying on one of the pairs of trousers when George arrived gasping for air. He looked at the pair of beige cords lying on mattress, they certainly weren't his. He looked at the pair Ronald was zipping up – they weren't his either. Now he was stuck with wearing someone else's. Was this torment never going to end? And he still had to phone the caterers and plead with them to stay put until he got to Nailsea. Surely it wouldn't matter if the Rotary Club's pensioners' supper dance was served a bit late for once.

Heaving a sigh of relief, he tore off the skirt and tights and pulled on the cords. They clashed horribly with his light grey suit jacket so he decided to keep the navy jumper on, it looked marginally better even if the sleeve was pulling off at the back.

Going back downstairs he glanced into Caroline's bedroom, which he still hadn't sorted out, and saw to his relief a phone on her bedside table. With adrenaline slopping about in his stomach he punched in the number and waited. The ansaphone message said his call was important and to leave his name and number.

He slumped on Caroline's bed, which before today he could never have imagined doing, but now felt normal. It was over, he should never have given into temptation. As a church warden he should have known better. He debated whether to go home and confess all, but that would mean saying goodbye to the money and his only hope now was to find another caterer. He forced himself to go downstairs.

Chapter 47

Still seething over Nicole, Marigold was doing her best to flirt with Charles - with little success. 'You're supposed to be my lover,' she hissed, 'now act like one.' When that didn't work, she snapped at Nicole and asked her to go and get her wrap as she was feeling chilly.

Charles immediately said he would go and get it, which enraged her even more and she snapped at him instead and told him not to bother.

Glancing round the room her eyes alighted on Alan and she walked across to him. 'So, you're now the vicar, are you?' She leaned in closer pressing her ample bosom against his arm and whispered, 'You do know you are madly in love with me, don't you?'

Alan jumped back as if stung. 'No, I'm not.'

'It's in the script darling, so start acting,' and Marigold wrapped herself round him like a boa constrictor.

Across the room Ronald was trying to remember where he'd seen the vicar before, then it hit him. As Dickie topped up his wine glass he hissed, 'That's the guy who kidnapped me. Now perhaps you'll believe me.' Still worried that Dickie might dock his wages, he insisted that Dickie should go and confront him.

But Dickie had already noticed that Alan was nervous of Maddie and now, clutched to Marigold's bosom, was positively wide-eyed with terror. 'Don't be daft Ronald, he couldn't kidnap a cushion.'

Tom watched everyone and tried to remember what was being said, but they were all talking at once. Then he had a brainwave. Excusing himself he went to the library and got the tape recorder. With it hidden under his jacket he sat down next to his wife and then surreptitiously eased it out and manage to push it behind the settee. Now he would be able to listen at his leisure later on.

But no sooner had he got the recorder in place than Dickie announced lunch was served and would they all come into the dining room.

The thought of food animated them all again and there was a quick dash next door where Alan found himself squeezed between Marigold who constantly tried to flirt with him, and Freda who gave him her full and frank views on all that was wrong with the ordination of women.

When Freda wasn't bending Alan's ear, Jack was trying to bend hers. Having discovered she ran a private school he was convinced she needed an impressionist painting to hang in the school hall. 'I can get you a very tasty little Van Gogh, you know him what done the sunflowers,' and when she didn't respond, he added, 'went mad and cut his ear off.'

'I know who you mean, but no.'

But Jack didn't give up that easily. 'Yeah, right he is a bit in yer face, but I've got a Monet what'd suit you down to the ground,' and added, 'he done a lot paintings of ponds.'

Freda tried to make it as plain as possible. 'School funds do not run to buying a Monet either, whether with ponds in it or not.'

Opposite Jack, Maddie was trying to answer Sergeant Cowden's questions. Although everyone else were now on first name terms, Tom insisted on being called by his full, police title on the basis that he would get better results in his interviews if he kept a professional distance from the other guests, including his wife.

'Oh, I don't think I can give you much information, officer, except it's usually the butler who does it.'

Next to Maddie, Edna and Angela debated the relative merits of Edna's quiches with Angela being unable to decide between the red onion and spinach, or the blue cheese and broccoli so had a piece of each.

Across from Marigold, Charles watched with amusement her efforts to entangle Alan in an amorous conversation.

And Ronald, as befitting his status as Bishop, sat at the head of the table smiling at everyone. He'd even managed a passable grace before everyone sat down.

George and Nicole were kept busing serving the guests, although George noted Nicole spent a lot of time leaning over Charles' shoulder to pass him food which he could easily have reached for himself, leaving George to do most of the work.

Nicole's attentiveness to Charles did not go unnoticed by Marigold either and she was getting angrier by the minute. And the angrier Marigold got the funnier Nicole found it.

Jack had given up on trying to get rid of his Monet to Freda, which was probably just as well as '*Duckweed in a Ditch at Giverny*' hadn't been one of his better ideas. He looked across the table at Maddie and started chatting to her instead. After all she did have the most wonderful hands, his neck had never felt better.

Finally, when everyone had their plates piled with food, George was allowed to sit down and have something to eat, but he'd no sooner helped himself to a corned beef sandwich and a piece of quiche when the doorbell rang.

'Can you get that George.'

He glared at Dickie who was sitting opposite end of the table to Ronald and was much nearer the door. The bell rang again, this time longer and angrier. Keeping his fingers crossed it was the caterers at long last he pushed back his chair.

As soon as he opened the door, he jumped back two feet and debated whether to slam it shut. His wife was standing there and he fully expected her to launch a verbal if not physical attack on him. Instead, she flung herself into his arms sobbing her heart out.

He gingerly patted her back, recent experience meant he was familiar with her mood swings and the need to act with caution. 'There, there, dear, what's happened?'

'The wedding's off, that's what's happened?' And her tears increased.

George immediately thought it was because the caterers had rung her and cancelled. 'We can find another company to do the food.'

She pulled away and glared at him, 'It's not the caterers you idiot, it's Lisa, she's broken off the engagement.'

George tried hard to look sad and bereft. He struggled to contort his features into a suitable expression of disbelief and disappointment. He tried to think of some comforting words for the crushed woman standing on the doorstep. But he couldn't because inside he was punching the air and shouting 'Yeeees.' Not only was he let off the hook for the morning's cock-up he'd never liked Lisa's fiancé anyway.

'Don't you want to know why?'

George wanted to say not really, instead he said, 'Of course, dear.'

'He wants to wear his Liverpool strip to the wedding, and his best man.'

George was horrified, 'How ridiculous, two grown men dressed as footballers - we'd be a laughing stock.' He had completely forgotten he'd spent half the morning running round dressed as a woman.

'You must go straight round and talk to him.' His wife started crying again.

'I can't…not at the moment.'

The tears stopped in a nanosecond to be replaced by another glare, 'Why not? Surely the cleaners can't still be here?' She stepped closer, 'Doesn't your daughter's happiness come first?'

'Yes of course it does dear…is she very upset?'

'That's not the point.'

'No of course not dear.'

She started crying again, 'And now we've lost the deposit on the buffet.'

George was about to say he hadn't actually paid it when it struck him - would she be pleased he still had the money or furious that he hadn't done the one thing she'd asked him to do that morning, there was no telling these days. 'Ummm…'

She stepped back and glared at him, 'How did you get to Nailsea, you never came back for the car?'

'Ah…Alan took me…his car was here and I thought it would be quicker.'

'So why didn't you come straight home afterwards instead of coming back here?'

George thought the Spanish Inquisition could have learned a thing or two about interrogation techniques from his wife. But a germ of an idea had crept into his head where he could come up smelling of roses.

'But none of that matters now dear, because I am going to go straight to Nailsca and insist they pay me back the money.'

'And if they won't?'

'I shall refuse to leave until they do.'

His wife brightened up immediately, 'We'll go together.'

'Ah. No…no, Lisa needs her mother at a moment like this, so you walk home and leave the car here for me.' When she still hesitated, he added, 'Just leave everything to me dear, everything is going to be fine. Now off you go.' As he watched her head down the drive, he decided to buy her a little present with some of the money. Then he headed back to the dining room with a spring in his step.

When Dickie wanted to know who was at the door, he said, 'Just my wife, everything's fine.' And he beamed round the round the room at everyone. 'Just fine. Alan can I get you some more wine?'

Having heard George's wife screaming down the phone at him earlier, Dickie was surprised George was still able to walk let alone pour out more wine.

Chapter 48

Jack was gazing at Maddie when he was hit with a sudden pain in his chest. He looked at Edna's quiche and decided not to risk a third piece. Delicious as it was, pastry played havoc with his digestion system, which was already in a delicate state.

He reached for a piece of cake instead and quickly swallowed an antiacid pill, but the pain didn't go away. Then he realised the room had grown silent around him and was blurred at the edges - all he could see was Maddie, glowing as if lit by a dozen candles. Then it hit him - he was in love.

In the ten seconds it took to finish a piece of Edna's fruit cake he had abandoned a career of forgery to take up designing cards with fluffy cats and dogs and naff verses.

Tom had given up trying to interrogate Maddie, who was gazing adoringly across the table at one of his main suspects, and was happily questioning Angela, who unaccustomed to so much attention, had told him her life story starting from her earliest memories aged two years and a half.

Which gave Freda and Edna a chance to bond across the table while enjoying Edna's fruitcake. Freda decided the weekend was turning out to be quite enjoyable after all.

Alan was starting to relax. Marigold had stopped squeezing his knee under the table, Freda had stopped bending his ear and even George had stopped glaring at him and poured him some more wine.

He finished his second piece of quiche, a luxury unheard of at home, and then helped himself to some pineapple souffle. He was sure Caroline was having a lovely time in Oxford and would never know how he had saved her. Perhaps one day he'd tell her.

Dickie was crossing the hall to make the coffee when the front door opened to reveal a young woman carrying a holdall. He quickly ran through in his mind the missing guests and concluded she was one half of the honeymoon couple. 'Mrs Harding?'

'No, I'm not – but more to the point, who the heck are you?'

George couldn't understand why Dickie was taking so long to get the coffee, but such was his euphoria he started collecting up the dirty crockery without being asked.

And promptly dropped the lot when he saw who was following Dickie into the dining room.

At the same moment, Alan jumped up, knocked his knee on the table and sent the remains of his pineapple souffle flying into Marigold's lap.

She also jumped up, screaming obscenities.

Freda jumped up and shouted, 'Don't use language like that in front of ladies.'

And for a few moments there was pandemonium. Ronald waded in, in defence of Marigold, Alan and George tried to explain, Tom surreptitiously took notes, Charles and Nicole tried not to laugh and Jack and Maddie gazed into each other's eyes and never heard a word.

When Dickie was finally able to calm things down, he pulled out a large envelope, stuffed with money. 'This weekend was to help raise money for the church roof fund so I have great pleasure in handing over five hundred pounds to Caroline Timberlake, the vicar of this parish.'

As soon as he'd given the money to Caroline he turned to George and added, 'And Caroline particularly asked me to thank you George for not only inviting me to put on this weekend, but taking part as well.' He then asked everyone to put their hands together, which they did with various degrees of enthusiasm.

Above the sound of the applause could be heard an anguished, 'Noooooooooo'.

Epilogue

George didn't leave the weekend empty handed - Dickie paid him, Alan and Nicole for taking part. And before he could offer to resign from the prestigious golf club, he was offered his money back because a friend of the chairman was desperate to join and needed the slot. So, he told his wife the deposit had been refunded and he going to take her on a luxury cruise instead.

Alan became Caroline's hero when she learned about the Bishop's visit and how he had saved the day. They were married the following year in a service take by Bishop Herbert and attended by Henrietta, Flora – under duress from Henrietta – and surprisingly Freda and Angela. After spending the weekend with Caroline, they completely changed their minds about the ordination of women and thought it was the best thing since slice bread. His mother has never forgiven him and neither has Ping.

Dickie continues to hold Murder Mystery Weekends, including one at Kingsford Manor, which was not a financial success owing to several of the guests issuing lawsuits against Henrietta's aunt - an inveterate collector of other people's possessions. So, Henrietta and family are still lunching on sardines.

Charles got a small, but long-running role in a television soap filmed in London, where he and Nicole have a trendy flat. They visit Kingsford regularly - although Charles is still wary of his father-in-law - and they were able to take part in 'Murder at the Manor'.

Angela and Freda also went to 'Murder at the Manor' along with Angela's daughter Barbara, and had a brilliant time. They never received a reply from the Archbishop.

Ronald and Marigold moved in together, to save money, and continue to hurl insults at each other from the comfort of their own home. Ronald got a divorce, but never told Marigold – once bitten twice shy.

Herbert never told Flora how he was able to start the Rover without the keys, but he has never risked it again. And Flora was so pleased to have the car back in one piece she didn't pursue the subject. One benefit of his escapades - he has had no further blackouts and his blood pressure is now normal so he can drive himself around.

Maddie and Jack Albright also got married and they too went to 'Murder at the Manor' where Jack was almost tempted to try to sell Henrietta one of his forgeries, just to keep his hand in. But he doesn't need the money because he has become an expert in how to spot forgeries, including his own, and is often on television - and it has even been mooted that he could one day present the Antiques Road Show.

Tom successfully solved the crime at the Vicarage, by deducing it was the Vicar who murdered the Hon Giles Forsythe and not the butler. When he returned to Devon, he wrote his memoirs of life on the beat, and has become a popular speaker at clubs, groups and societies. Edna always goes with him to work his slide show and has collected dozens more quiche recipes, which she is hoping to turn into a book.

THE END

,

Printed in Great Britain
by Amazon

68176739R00169